THE UNEXPECTED?

WHISPERS OF SHANTI VILLA

MRUNALINI PHADE

Made with ♥ on the Notion Press Platform
www.notionpress.com

To my beloved parents, (Kishor and Pratibha Phade),

Your unwavering love, encouragement, and support have been the guiding light on my journey as a writer. From the earliest scribbles to the completion of this book, you have stood by me with boundless patience and endless belief in my dreams.

Thank you for nurturing my creativity, instilling in me the values of perseverance and dedication, and for being my greatest champions. This book is as much yours as it is mine, a testament to the love and sacrifices you have made for me.

Remembering

B N Behera,

My father-in-law whose warmth and wisdom illuminated every step of my journey. Though you are no longer with us, your spirit lives on in the words of this book, a tribute to the love and inspiration you instilled in us all. Forever in our hearts.

Contents

Disclaimer

"This work of fiction, The Unexpected ?'Whispers of Shanti Villa,' is purely a product of the author's imagination and is not intended to depict any real events, persons, or entities. Any resemblance to actual persons, living or dead, or actual events is purely coincidental. The views and opinions expressed in this book are those of the characters and do not necessarily reflect those of the author. The author and publisher do not endorse or condone any illegal or unethical behavior depicted in this work. All rights reserved. No part of this book may be reproduced or transmitted in any form or by any means, electronic or mechanical, without permission from the author or the publisher."

CHAPTER ONE

The Call

As the first rays of sunlight gently crept through the window, Deven's eyelids fluttered open, pulling him from the embrace of slumber. With a resigned sigh, he swung his legs over the edge of the bed, his feet meeting the cool floor. The monotonous routine awaited – the hiss of the shower, the clink of his shaving tools, and the attire neatly chosen from the closet. In these early hours, the world outside remained a distant hum, while Deven prepared to step into the bustling current of another day at the office.

In his early thirties, Deven Kulkarni bore the weight of experience in the lines etched upon his forehead and the subtle hints of wisdom hidden behind his eyes. With a physique that hinted at an unspoken dedication to fitness, he moved with an air of understated confidence, his stride purposeful yet not hurried. His dark, slightly tousled hair seemed to mirror the controlled chaos of his life, falling just short of his brow as if to shield his thoughts from the world. Deven's wardrobe exuded a blend of professionalism and comfort, reflecting his life within the corporate realm. Crisp shirts and well-fitted trousers formed the armor he donned each day, a uniform of sorts for navigating the intricacies of boardrooms and client meetings.

Behind the veneer of his routine existence lay a story of loss and resilience. With the untimely departure of his parents, Deven had found himself leading a solitary path. His apartment in Pune, Maharashtra adorned with minimalistic furnishings and a few cherished mementos, was both a sanctuary and a reminder of his independence. The city's bustling energy outside his window was in stark contrast to the stillness he cultivated within. From the early morning ritual of brewing his favorite blend of coffee to the final moments of the evening spent immersed in a book, tinkering with his guitar, or watching web series each day followed the tracks of familiarity.

Yet, as the pages of Deven's life continued to turn, he remained unknowingly poised at the edge of change. The rhythm of his routine was about to be disrupted by forces he couldn't anticipate. Little did he know, this seemingly ordinary morning held the potential to unravel the tapestry of his routine existence, setting him on a course toward unexpected encounters and transformative revelations.

That call he received on Friday morning was going to change is entire life and how.

In the midst of his hurried morning routine, Deven's phone suddenly erupted with a sharp trill, its screen illuminating with an incoming call from an unknown number. Juggling his keys and a half-finished cup of coffee, he shot a quick glance at the caller ID before a sigh of impatience escaped his lips. Time was slipping through his fingers, and he couldn't afford any distractions. With a dismissive press of a button, he silenced the call, watching the phone's display dim back into darkness.

A short while later, amidst the chaotic rhythm of his work, Deven's phone buzzed insistently, drawing his attention to a new message notification. Curiosity piqued, he unlocked his device and his eyes scanned the screen. The message, succinct yet intriguing, read:

"Hello Deven,

Apologies for the abrupt attempt to reach you. My name is Sachin Dhar, and I believe have something very important to discuss with you. I represent M& P Associates, a Legal Firm. I would like to discuss an important matter which will surely benefit you. If you're open to it, I propose a meeting at my office tomorrow at 2 PM. Location Pin is sent with the message understand your time is valuable, but I assure you this meeting could be a turning point. Kindly consider my invitation.

Best regards, Sachin Dhar, Solicitor for M & P Legal "

In the midst of Deven's ordinary life, where legal intricacies were nothing more than distant concepts, an unexpected message brought a twist. He had never encountered a lawyer, much less understood the nuances between a lawyer, and solicitor. These terms were mere jargon to him, lost in a world he had never explored. However, driven by an insatiable curiosity and a desire to unravel the mystery, he composed a reply that would forever alter his trajectory. "I will be there," he typed, his keystrokes carrying a blend of anticipation and intrigue, unknowingly stepping into a realm he had never imagined. Little did Deven know that his response would initiate a chain of events that would unravel his perception of the legal world, intertwining his fate with the complexities he was about to confront.

As Deven arrived at the designated location, a sense of anticipation gripped him. The exterior of the law office exuded an air of sophistication, its grand facade hinting at the gravity of the matters discussed within.

Stepping into the well-furnished office, Deven was welcomed by Mr. Dhar with a warm smile. The room exuded an aura of professionalism, adorned with shelves of leather-bound tomes and a mahogany desk. Mr. Dhar, man in his fifties extended his hand, his eyes reflecting gratitude through his rimless glasses as he thanked Deven for taking the time to meet him.

Mr. Dhar: (Smiling) You must be curious why I asked you to meet at my office, and what you have to do with any legality?

Deven: (Nervous chuckle) Well, yes, Mr. Dhar. It's not every day that someone gets a message from a prominent lawyer asking them to come in for a chat. And, you know, it's been said that a wise person avoids going to police stations and lawyers, so I am a little curious and nervous at the same time.

Mr. Dhar: (Chuckling) I can understand that. Please, have a seat. First of all, I want to assure you that you're not in any kind of trouble. You're not here as a suspect or anything of that sort. Do you know who Mrs. Asha Joshi is?

Deven: Never heard this name before

Mr.Dhar: So as you don't know who Mrs Joshi is.I need to tell you few things in detail. So, brace yourself.

In the vast tapestry of our world, countless individuals remain shrouded in anonymity, hidden from our awareness like stars in the daytime sky. These enigmatic souls, who deliberately or involuntarily dwell in the shadows, hold within them stories untold, aspirations unseen, and emotions unfelt by the rest of us. Their isolation might be a result of a deliberate retreat from societal connection, or it could stem from circumstances beyond their control. Yet, it's precisely in their unexpected emergence or unanticipated actions that the course of our lives can be forever altered. A chance encounter, a random act of kindness, or an unforeseen event can bridge the chasm between their seclusion and our world, leaving an indelible mark that reminds us of the intricate interplay between the known and the mysterious, the seen and the unseen. I know you have no interest in my philosophy so I come directly to the point.

Mrs Joshi Used to stay in a Vada (bungalow) near Shivaji Nagar, model colony Pune.

Deven interrupted, what do you mean by she used to stay?

She passed away few months ago, Said Mr. Dhar. She used to stay in that vada (bungalow) by herself, she was of about 67,68 years old when she passed away.

Deven-What happened to her then? Was she ill?

No, she wasn't ill, Mr.Dhar replied,infact she used to manage her entire house by herself. Only a lady who was her house help who used to clean the house, mop the floor and do certain other household chores used to come daily between 8 , 8.30ish.As Mrs Joshi used to lock the doors with an big iron lock from inside it used to take her 10 to 15 minutes daily to open it.But the door wasn't answered for more than half hour. She tried to call her on her landline number as Mrs.Joshi was not having any cellphone, after almost forty minutes, she panicked and called her husband who later called few neighbours near the bungalow which included the laundry guy ,kirana store owner who used to deliver groceries to Mrs Joshi and several other people who happened to know her. But no one dared to break the door as who would take the risk?

Finally, they called police, amidst growing concern for Mrs. Joshi, a respected senior citizen within the community, the police found themselves compelled to forcefully breach the imposing door of her bungalow. Fearing a potential medical crisis, their urgency drove them to apply substantial force, their repeated strikes echoing through the quiet neighborhood. The door, unyielding and fortified, proved to be a formidable barrier, demanding a persistent and forceful assault to surmount. After a series of unrelenting efforts, the tenacity of the police prevailed, and with a resounding crash, the door yielded, granting them access to the interior of the bungalow. The culmination of their determined endeavors provided a sense of relief, as they could now attend to whatever situation lay inside.

To their surprise, upon gaining entry, the police were met with an unsettling discovery – Mrs. Joshi was missing from the premises of her bungalow. An air of perplexity hung heavy as both Police and concerned neighbors meticulously combed through every nook and cranny of the house as well as the garden outside the house. Their search extended to the upper floor and even the storage room, attic nestled at the pinnacle of the house, but their efforts yielded no trace of her whereabouts. The sense of mystery deepened, prompting questions as to the nature of her sudden disappearance.

With the initiation of a missing person case, a rigorous investigation was set into motion. Every corner, wardrobe, and room of Mrs. Joshi's bungalow became a canvas for the meticulous search, an attempt to unearth any semblance of a clue. In her bedroom, among her personal stuff on the side table, the investigators discovered a note. Penned in her own handwriting, it had a poignant message:

"I don't know what is happening to me or what my destiny has planned for me; I am scared. If anything should befall me, please seek out my estranged cousin, Usha. She is the sole remaining blood relation I have, and I hereby designate her as the rightful heir to this property. The uncertainty of her survival troubles me, but if she is no more, kindly transfer the property to her closest kin. There's only one condition: that he or she must not inhabit this house."

This enigmatic revelation cast a new light on the situation, invoking a sense of intrigue that would guide the unfolding investigation.

Intrigued and slightly apprehensive, Deven sat in the lawyer's office, his senses tuned to every word that Mr. Dhar was saying. Each syllable carried a weight of mystery, and Deven's curiosity only deepened as the questions tumbled forth. He leaned in, his expression a mix of confusion and concern, as he implored Mr. Dhar and asked him, It's Indeed very sad but What is my connection to all this Sir? how I am related to Mrs Joshi? Every detail, every nuance of the conversation, felt like a puzzle piece he needed to fit together.

Deven,Mr.Dhar said in a very sharp voice. You are the rightful heir to Mrs. Joshi's entire estate. Her estranged cousin Usha, she mentioned in her note and also her will is your grandmother Mrs. Kusum Patwardhan. As she is no more and you're the only person who is directly closely related to her as per our investigation and order of court.

Suddenly, As Mr. Dhar continued to unveil the pieces of the puzzle, Deven's mind raced to assemble the newfound information. The revelation that Mrs. Usha was his maternal grandmother, whose name was changed after marriage as Mrs. Kusum Patwardhan, sent shockwaves through him. He vividly remembered the fragments of conversations his mother had shared about her estranged family – tales of loss, and a grandmother who had passed away long before his time. The realization struck him like a lightning bolt, connecting the dots between his fragmented family history and the present moment. Deven's upbringing in the hostel after he lost his parents and the subsequent demands of his job had distanced him from his roots. The hazy memories of his parents' tragic accident left him with a void that he hadn't fully comprehended until now. The lawyer's office suddenly felt like a crossroads, where the past and the present collided. Questions abounded in his mind, clamoring for answers he had never thought to seek.

As Deven's mind continued to wrestle with the sudden turn of events, a seed of doubt began to sprout. What if this was all an elaborate scam? The thought nagged at him, feeding his skepticism and prompting him to question Mr. Dhar's motives. Could this be an attempt to lure him into a web of deceit, all under the guise of an unexpected inheritance? He couldn't ignore the possibility that Mr. Dhar might stand to benefit financially from orchestrating such a scheme. What evidence did Mr. Dhar have to support the claims he had made? The absence of concrete proof gnawed at Deven's trust. The initial sense of curiosity was now tinged with a growing wariness. Deven knew that he needed to proceed with caution, to seek validation beyond just words. His mind was set on unearthing the truth, one piece at a time, even if it meant facing the stark reality that this could all be an intricately woven deception.

As Mr. Dhar began to address the doubts swirling in Deven's mind, his words carried a veneer of understanding. The seasoned solicitor acknowledged the incredulity that Deven was experiencing and attempted to shed light on the intricacies of the situation. He leaned forward, his expression earnest as he explained the complex process surrounding unclaimed properties. Mr. Dhar's voice resonated with a mix of empathy and assurance.

"Deven," he began, "I fully understand your doubts. It's only natural given the circumstances. Let me provide you with some additional details that might help you see the larger picture. When properties go unclaimed and end up in the hands of the government, it's a meticulous process that involves investigation and scrutiny. These properties are then entrusted to custodians, individuals appointed by the government to manage and maintain them. Mrs. Joshi's case is no exception. She left behind substantial investments and savings that are more than sufficient to cover the necessary expenses."

Deven's mind absorbed the information as he processed the intricacies of the situation. Mr. Dhar continued, "As the custodian, it's my responsibility to locate and connect with the rightful heir, which in this case, is you. I assure you, my intention is to fulfil this duty with utmost integrity. However, I understand your concerns about my involvement. Rest assured, the funds necessary for the legal proceedings and searches were allocated from the investments left behind by Mrs. Joshi. My role is to ensure that her wishes are carried out and that her legacy is properly passed on."

A sceptical thought flitted across Deven's mind, echoing his earlier apprehension. Why would Mr. Dhar be so generous and helpful? Was there a hidden motive behind his actions? As Deven mulled over these thoughts, he couldn't help but wonder if this display of assistance was a guise for financial gain. Nevertheless, he recognized the need for further investigation and clarity.

Listening intently, Deven finally spoke, "Mr. Dhar, I appreciate your explanation, and I understand the process better now. However, given the circumstances, it's only natural for me to exercise caution. I will require more concrete evidence and transparency before fully committing to this issue."

Mr. Dhar nodded understandingly, his demeanour maintaining its professionalism. "Of course, Deven. Your caution is wise, and I respect your desire for transparency. I'm prepared to provide you with all the necessary documentation and details to put your mind at ease. Let's work together to ensure that you have a complete and accurate understanding of your inheritance and the responsibilities that come with it, however as we promised to be transparent with each other, I will be expecting some appropriate fees for my support and services. As you don't have to worry about the documentation and you will not need to visit the government offices for anything but for signing the documents. I will save lot of your efforts ,and in return

I will expect an appropriate amount .

So what is the exact valuation of the entire property ? Deven asked with curiosity .

As Mr. Dhar shared the estimated breakdown of the property's value, a mixture of astonishment and apprehension rippled through Deven. The numbers were far beyond what he had ever anticipated. The savings and investments, valued at around 5 crore, the collection of precious items worth nearly 2 Crores, and the bungalow along with the expansive plot valued at 10 crore – a sum that left Deven momentarily speechless. The grand total, amounting to approximately 17,18 crores, painted a picture of an inheritance that was both remarkable and overwhelming.

As the figures settled in his mind, Deven's thoughts raced. The monetary value was beyond what he could have imagined, yet it was tempered by the realization that this inheritance carried not only financial responsibility but also a deep historical and emotional weight. He looked at Mr. Dhar, his expression a mixture of awe and uncertainty.

"Mr. Dhar, these numbers are staggering," Deven said, his voice a blend of reverence and apprehension. "I'm still trying to wrap my head around all of this. The legacy is immense, and I want to make sure I handle it with the respect it deserves."

Mr. Dhar nodded, his eyes reflecting understanding. "I completely understand, Deven. It's a significant responsibility that comes with various layers. As your solicitor and guide in this process, I'm here to support you every step of the way. While the financial value is substantial, remember that the intangible aspects –

the stories, the history – are just as valuable. Take your time to absorb everything and let me know how you'd like to proceed."

Deven took a deep breath, his mind grappling with the weight of the situation. The legacy that had suddenly come into his life was vast, both in terms of its material value and the emotional ties it carried. The conversation had brought him face-to-face with a reality he had never envisioned, and now he had to determine how he would navigate this newfound inheritance and the responsibilities it entailed.

Mr. Dhar nodded understandingly at Deven's response. "Deven, I appreciate your transparency and concern. I completely understand your stance, and I want to assure you that my priority is to ensure that the legal proceedings are carried out smoothly and ethically. Your inheritance is my main focus, and any fees or costs associated with the process will be deducted from the inheritance itself. There is no need for any upfront payments or advances."

Deven's sense of cautious relief was palpable as Mr. Dhar's words reassured him. "Thank you for understanding, Mr. Dhar. This situation is new to me, and I want to make sure that I'm making the right decisions. I believe that if everything is done according to the proper legal procedures and timelines, then the financial aspects will naturally fall into place."

Mr. Dhar offered a reassuring smile. "You're absolutely right, Deven. I commend your diligence in approaching this matter thoughtfully. Rest assured, I will handle all the necessary legalities diligently, and I will keep you informed at every step. Your concerns and comfort are of utmost importance."

With the understanding between them firmly established, Deven felt a sense of relief mingled with a renewed determination to navigate this journey carefully. As they continued to discuss the practicalities and details, he realized that this newfound inheritance was not just a financial windfall, but a doorway to uncovering a part of his family's history and legacy that he had never anticipated. And as he delved deeper, he knew that he was on the brink of a profound and transformative chapter in his life.

CHAPTER TWO

23/2 Shanti Villa

The following week proved to be busy week for Deven. With a newfound purpose and a mission at hand, he navigated the bustling streets of his city, juggling variety of tasks that seemed to demand his attention all at once. From visiting government offices to signing legal documents, from meeting with tax advisors to discussing the intricate details with Mr. Dhar, each day brought forth new challenges and revelations.

Deven's commitment to this journey was evident not just to himself but to those around him. His colleagues and superiors at the office noted his focused determination as he skilfully handled his responsibilities before his leave. The news of Deven seeking time off for an entire week was met with surprise, yet the HR department readily granted his request, recognizing his dedicated work ethic and his rarely taken leaves over his five-year tenure.

With a carefully planned schedule and a clear sense of purpose, Deven embarked on this week-long journey with a mix of anticipation and resolve. His interactions with various professionals and authorities were marked by a thirst for knowledge and a meticulous attention to detail. As he delved deeper into the intricacies of legal proceedings and financial matters, Deven's once sceptical outlook was gradually being replaced by a growing confidence in the path he was treading.

Through the hectic days and late nights spent poring over documents, Deven's mind occasionally drifted to the stories that were waiting to be unearthed within the walls of the inherited property. He imagined the tales that echoed through its corridors, the memories etched into its foundation. The property wasn't just a collection of structures and possessions; it held the essence of a lineage that was now becoming entwined with his own.

As the week progressed, Deven's determination remained unwavering, his actions speaking volumes about his commitment to unravelling the truth behind this unexpected inheritance. And as the days unfurled, he was on the cusp of stepping into a realm that promised not only financial prosperity, but a profound connection to his past and the untold stories that awaited his discovery.

The morning of the day Deven had been waiting for finally arrived, ushering in a sense of both excitement and trepidation. He had navigated through a maze of legalities, financial assessments, and paperwork, and now the time had come for the tangible connection to his inheritance. As he made his way to the property, a mixture of anticipation and wonder filled his thoughts.

With the keys now securely in his possession, Deven felt a surge of excitement as he started on his first journey to Mrs. Joshi's house. The address, "23/2 Shanti Villa," held a sense of mystery and promise, and the prospect of stepping into a property that was now intricately linked to his own history filled him with a mixture of eagerness and wonder.

The short uber drive of around 5,7 kilometers from his place of residence to the new property felt like a journey bridging the past and the present. As uber cab glided through the streets, his thoughts meandered between his expectations and the unknown that awaited him. The cityscape shifted, gradually giving way to a quieter neighborhood, and he found himself facing the entrance of Shanti Villa.

Standing before the bungalow at 23/2 Shanti Villa, Deven's initial impression was one of surprise. The image he had in his mind didn't quite match the reality before him. The bungalow, constructed from sturdy stones, stood as a testament to its age, revealing a timeless charm that spoke of a bygone era. The nameplate, "23/2 Shanti Villa," showed signs of rust, hinting at the passage of time and the stories that had unfolded within these walls.

As Deven look in the details, he couldn't help but be struck by the house's impeccable condition. Despite its age, it exuded an air of solidity and durability. The architecture, though old-fashioned, bore an elegance that transcended trends. The entrance gate, a testament to a time when grandeur was a priority, welcomed him with open arms, as if extending an invitation to uncover the secrets it held.

With a mix of curiosity and reverence, Deven stepped inside. The interiors of the bungalow seemed to echo the exterior's theme of timeless grace. Ornate details adorned the walls, and vintage furniture was arranged in a way that told stories of gatherings and conversations from years gone by. The air was infused with a sense of nostalgia, as if the essence of the past lingered in every corner.

Deven's initial surprise transformed into a sense of appreciation. While the bungalow might not have matched his preconceived notions, it possessed a character that was unique and captivating. As he explored further, he envisioned the potential for modern touches that would seamlessly blend with the bungalow's inherent charm, creating a space that honoured the past while embracing the present.

He realized that this unexpected inheritance was not just about property or financial gain; it was a gift, a connection to a woman named Mrs. Joshi who had unknowingly left an indelible mark on his life.

With each step he took through the bungalow, Deven felt a growing appreciation for the woman who had once called this place home. He imagined her life, her experiences, and the decisions she had made that had eventually led to this moment. Mrs. Joshi's legacy was more than just a physical property; it was a bridge between generations, a link to a past he was now a part of.

Deven's exploration of the bungalow led him to discover its various facets, each offering a glimpse into the history and lifestyle of the past. the property had two floors. And on the top, there was a pyramid shaped attic. there was no balcony to the bungalow but it had several windows which are now closed.

Deven was at ground floor, the ground floor had a big hall next to it was a modular kitchen with all the modern facilities. a big dining hall with rectangle shaped dining table. on top of it was a huge chandelier. It also had a common washroom and a sink next to it. He now eventually moved to a room that held a particular significance—the pooja room. As he entered, he noticed the emptiness that now defined the space. The room that had once been a place for devotion and prayer was now devoid of the items that would have once adorned it. The absence of religious artifacts and symbols created a sense of void, a quiet reminder of the changes that had taken place.

Deven stood there for a moment, the emptiness of the room prompting reflections on the passage of time and the evolution of traditions. He thought about the rituals and moments of solace that must have occurred within these walls, the diya that would have been lit, the incense that would have wafted through the air. Deven's mind was a mix of emotions. He contemplated the changes that time had brought, the transformations that inevitably occur as one generation passes the torch to the next. The emptiness of the room served as a reminder that while the physical artifacts might change, the spirit of devotion and connection endures.

He stumbled upon a discovery that added a new layer of understanding to the history of the bungalow. Two large old photo frames adorned the wall, their presence evoking a sense of nostalgia and intrigue. The names inscribed at the bottom of the frames—Mrs. Shanti Joshi and Mr. Anand Joshi—offered a glimpse into the identities of the individuals captured within the photographs.

The realization struck him: the bungalow was named after Mrs. Shanti Joshi. She was not just an anonymous figure from the past. The thought crossed Deven's mind that Mrs. Shanti Joshi might have been the mother-in-law of Mrs. Asha Joshi, possibly the same Mrs. Joshi who had passed away and left this inheritance to him

As Deven continued his exploration of the bungalow, he found himself standing before a row of three rooms on his left-hand side. These rooms, shrouded in darkness due to closed windows, piqued his curiosity. The contrast between the well-lit areas he had previously traversed and the dimness of these rooms added an air of mystery to his journey.

Intrigued, Deven approached the rooms and cautiously pushed open one of the doors. As the door swung open, sunlight streamed into the room, casting a warm glow on the surfaces that had been hidden from view. The scene that unfolded before him was a blend of the past and the present, a mixture of forgotten spaces and the potential for transformation. The room held remnants of its former inhabitants—a sense of life frozen in it.

As he ascended the staircase to visit upper floor, a feeling of anticipation mingled with the creaking of the steps beneath his feet. He found himself standing before a door, an unexpected barrier that separated the upper and lower levels of the bungalow. The presence of a gaint lock on the door deepened the intrigue, igniting Deven's curiosity further.

"Why was this connection closed off?" Deven wondered aloud, his thoughts echoing in the dimly lit space. "And why lock it?"

The idea that Mrs. Joshi had intentionally closed off this passage intrigued him. Deven contemplated the significance of this door. Was it merely a matter of practicality, a decision to restrict access between the floors? Or did it carry a deeper meaning, a deliberate choice to separate the spaces and the lives that unfolded within them?

His hand rested on the doorknob, his mind a whirlwind of questions. With a determined yet cautious motion, he found the Key for the lock to open it, he turned the knob. To his surprise, the door swung open, revealing a space that bridged the gap between the two floors. The air was still, a mixture of dust and the scent of time. Deven stepped into the space, his footsteps echoing softly. As he stood within the connecting corridor, he felt as though he was standing at the intersection of time, a place where the lives of generations intersected.

The locked door had been opened, both literally and metaphorically. The space between the two floors became a symbol of connection, a link between the lives that had once intertwined within this bungalow. And as Deven stood in the midst of this passage, he realized that the journey of discovery was not just about uncovering physical spaces, but also about unravelling the stories that were hidden behind closed doors, waiting to be unlocked.

CHAPTER THREE

Unveiling the shadows

The realization that Mrs. Joshi had no children brought a thought in Deven's situation. He was thinking of the implications of owning such a sizable house, especially for someone who lived alone.

As he walked through the upper floor, he began to see the pieces of the puzzle coming together. The upper floor appeared to be unused and locked away, its secrets hidden from view. Deven couldn't help but wonder if the decision to lock the upper floor was motivated by a desire for practicality or a deeper reason—one that was tied to memories, emotions, or stories that Mrs. Joshi might have wished to keep private.

As Deven stepped into the upper floor, it became immediately apparent that this space had been untouched by time for years. The atmosphere held a stillness, as if the passage of time had left its mark in a deliberate pause. The surroundings offered a vivid glimpse into the era when the bungalow was built—a world that seemed to exist parallel to the present. The old furniture that adorned the rooms told stories of a bygone time. Ornate wooden pieces stood as sentinels, guardians of the past, each bearing the patina of years. The craftsmanship of these relics spoke of an attention to detail and a dedication to quality that was characteristic of a different age.

Amid the rooms frozen in time, Deven's exploration brought him to a corner that held a treasure trove of knowledge and art—the library. The collection of rare books, neatly arranged on wooden shelves, beckoned him with an air of intellectual curiosity. Each book seemed to carry the weight of history, a testament to the intellectual pursuits that had taken place within these walls. The presence of antiques and paintings by renowned artists added a layer of artistic significance to the space. Each antique carried with it a sense of history, a glimpse into the aesthetics and tastes of a previous era. The paintings, with their intricate details and evocative strokes, transformed the walls into a gallery that told stories without words.

Among the rooms filled with remnants of the past, Deven's attention was drawn to a room that stood in stark contrast. Unlike the other spaces, this room was completely empty, its walls devoid of furnishings, its floors free from the traces of time. The emptiness was almost palpable, and it felt like a pause—a deliberate break from the clutter and memories that filled the rest of the floor.

As he stepped into the room, Deven was struck by the sense of disconnection it carried. It was as if this room was intentionally isolated from the rest of the upper floor, a space that existed in its own realm. The emptiness seemed to hold a question mark, an invitation to unravel the mystery of its purpose.

Deven's mind began to spin theories about the purpose of this room. Was it a place of retreat, where one could find solitude and respite from the demands of daily life? Or perhaps it held a specific purpose that had been forgotten with time? The disconnection from the rest of the floor only deepened the mystery, leaving him with more questions than answers.

Amid the emptiness of the room, Deven's eyes fell upon the solitary pieces of furniture—an old antique table and four chairs, all covered in a layer of dust. Despite the room's emptiness, these items seemed to stand as sentinels of a past era, a reminder that even in its bareness, this room had a story to tell.

And there he saw it, a sight that sent shivers down his spine, freezing him in place. His eyes widened as they locked onto the unmistakable marks imprinted in the layer of dust on the table. Handprints. But these were not ordinary handprints; they were distorted, elongated, the fingers splayed out like grotesque claws. The air in the room seemed to grow heavier, suffused with an unsettling energy that sent a chill through Deven's body.

His heart raced, and a knot of unease tightened in his stomach. The once-familiar room now felt alien, the atmosphere charged with an eerie tension that seemed to warp reality. The handprints, stark against the dust-covered surface, held an otherworldly quality that defied explanation.

As Deven's gaze remained fixed on the bizarre imprints, a sense of dread crept over him. The thought that someone—or something—had left those marks filled his mind, and his imagination conjured images of twisted figures lurking in the shadows. The notion that those distorted handprints might belong to an entity with malevolent intent sent a shiver down his spine.

A sense of being watched settled upon him, the very air vibrating with an unseen presence. The room, once a blank canvas awaiting meaning, now seemed to pulsate with an unsettling energy. Deven's breath grew shallow, his pulse quickening with each passing second.

He tore his gaze away from the table and surveyed the room, his senses on high alert. The once-empty chairs seemed to take on a different form, shadows dancing in the periphery of his vision. Every creak of the floorboards, every whisper of the curtains, heightened the tension that hung in the air like a heavy fog.

Deven felt a surge of fear, his instincts telling him that he was not alone in that room. The handprints on the table were a chilling reminder of the mysteries that shrouded the upper floor, the stories that were waiting to be unraveled. With his heart racing and his senses on edge, he slowly backed away from the table, leaving the room behind. The door closed with a soft click, and as he stepped back into the corridor, he couldn't shake the feeling that the presence he had sensed was still lingering, a spectral Specter in the dark recesses of the bungalow.

With trepidation, it was now time for Deven to venture into the attic, a space that held its own aura of mystery and foreboding. The weight of his previous encounter lingered, casting an unsettling shadow over his steps. His legs felt heavy, as if each footfall was a struggle against an invisible force that sought to hold him back.

As he was at the stairs leading to the attic, the air seemed to grow colder, the very atmosphere tinged with an unnatural chill. Deven's thoughts were a tumultuous whirlpool, a battleground between his determination and the lingering fear that the upper floor had ignited.

A voice within him whispered, urging him to turn back, to abandon his journey into the unknown. But he fought against the tendrils of doubt that threatened to ensnare him. "C'mon, Deven," he muttered to himself, his words a fervent mantra. "You can't be serious. Don't let fear control you. Let's get over with this "

Deven ascended the staircase leading to the attic, a sense of determination guided his steps. The shadows that had threatened to engulf him were now met with the resolve to uncover the mysteries that awaited him. His hand reached out for the light switch, and with a flick, a dim glow enveloped the staircase, casting a pale illumination on the path ahead.

The feeble light struggled against the darkness, creating a contrast that seemed to mirror the battle within Deven's own mind. But even as the dimness persisted, Deven's gaze was drawn to the attic door at the top of the stairs.

With each step he took, Deven willed himself to shed the apprehension that had taken hold. He knew that his imagination could conjure terrors where none existed, that the human mind was adept at weaving webs of fear from the shadows. As he reached the attic door, he took a deep breath, the inhale and exhale a rhythmic pulse of courage.

As he reached the top of the staircase, the light from the attic window enveloped him in a cocoon of radiance. The sunlight, filtered through dust particles in the air, created an ethereal ambiance that seemed to transcend the ordinary. The attic door stood before him, a portal to a world of secrets waiting to be unveiled.

In that moment, Deven's doubts began to dissipate, replaced by a newfound sense of purpose. The dim light of the staircase had led him to this point, where the sunlight from the attic's window served as a guiding force. He took a deep breath, his heart steadying, as he turned the doorknob and stepped into the attic. The attic sprawled before Deven like a forgotten realm, its secrets hidden beneath layers of dust and obscurity. The feeble light that filtered through the window painted eerie patterns on the floor, casting elongated shadows that danced like spectres in the corners. The air was heavy with the scent of age, a musty reminder of the passage of time.

As the sunlight beam cut through the gloom, Deven's gaze fell upon a chaotic landscape of old scraps and forgotten belongings. Broken furniture, rusted tools, and forgotten relics lay strewn across the floor like the discarded remnants of a forgotten past. Each piece seemed to carry a history of its own, an echo of lives long gone.

And then, amidst the debris, the sunlight illuminated something that made his heart skip a beat. Footprints—distinct, heavy marks that trailed across the dust-covered floor. It was as if something had been dragged across the attic, leaving an indelible trace of its passage. Deven's eyes followed the path, a knot of dread forming in his stomach as he imagined the weight and force required to create those tracks.

But that was not all. Alongside the footprints were handprints—some large, others small—stamped onto the surface as if imprinted by invisible hands. The sight was both eerie and perplexing, the imprints resembling claws more than fingers. The realization struck Deven like a bolt of lightning: whatever had created these marks was not human, not in any ordinary sense.

A chill ran down his spine, sending a shiver through his body. The room seemed to close in around him, the atmosphere becoming charged with a palpable tension. Deven's pulse quickened, his breath hitching in his throat as he tried to rationalize the inexplicable scene before him.

The footprints, the handprints—they were a puzzle that defied any logical explanation. The attic, once a space of forgotten artifacts, had become a canvas of the uncanny and the unsettling. As Deven stood in that dimly lit room, he felt a presence—something unseen but undeniably real. The shadows seemed to stir, as if whispering secrets that were beyond his comprehension. A chill ran through Deven's veins, his breath catching in his throat. The sensation of being watched was suffocating, an invisible weight that settled upon him with an ominous intensity.

Without hesitation, his instinct for self-preservation kicked in. Deven's trembling hand reached for the attic door, his fingers fumbling to grasp the doorknob. With a swift movement, he pulled the door shut behind him, the sound of the latch clicking into place a reassuring barrier against the unknown.

He stumbled backward, his heart pounding like a drum in his chest. The room he had hastily left behind now seemed to vibrate with an unsettling energy. The image of the figure watching from the stairs was etched into his mind, an indelible mark of fear.He immediately returned and almost ran towards the ground floor and locked the door which he opened with excitement and curiosity.

Deven stood there, in the dimly lit corridor, the echoes of his own heartbeat resounding in his ears like a primal drum. The rhythm was a testament to the adrenaline that had surged through his veins, His chest heaved as he finally released the breath he had been holding since his first encounter on the upper floor. The exhale was a release—a catharsis—as if expelling the pent-up tension that had built within him. The memories of the strange handprints, the distorted footprints, and the unsettling presence on the stairs all fused together into a whirlwind of emotions that now found their way to the surface.

With each heartbeat that gradually slowed, Deven regained his focus and his sense of self. The upper floor was a labyrinth of mysteries and fears, but he had braved its depths and emerged on the other side. The weight of the unknown still hung in the air, but his determination had carried him through the chilling encounters, and he knew that he could navigate whatever secrets the bungalow held.

Deven's thoughts swirled in a maelstrom of speculation, the enigmatic puzzle of Mrs. Joshi's disappearance haunting his every contemplation. The very idea that she had vanished while the doors of the bungalow remained locked from the inside was a conundrum that defied rational explanation. It was a mystery that tugged at the edges of his understanding, tempting him to delve deeper into the labyrinth of the upper floor. He couldn't help but empathize with her plight, imagining the unimaginable circumstances she might have faced.

The image of her, alone and facing the unknown, tugged at his heartstrings. What had compelled her to lock herself away, had she too encountered the unsettling handprints and the eerie presence that had sent shivers down his spine? Deven knew that he was standing at the precipice of a journey—one that would lead him deeper into the heart of the bungalow's enigma, and perhaps shed light on the fate of the woman who had become an enigmatic specter in his thoughts.

As Deven stepped out of the bungalow, his mind still entangled in the web of thoughts surrounding Mrs. Joshi's mysterious disappearance, his gaze caught on something unexpected. There, standing at the entrance gate, was an elderly woman—a stranger with a perplexed expression etched across her face. The lines of her features seemed to carry a lifetime of experiences, and her eyes bore a mix of curiosity and uncertainty.

The sight of the elderly woman immediately piqued Deven's interest. He couldn't shake the feeling that there might be a connection, a thread linking her to the enigmatic woman who had left an indelible mark on this house with her disappearance. The thought crossed his mind that this woman right here might possess answers to the questions that had been haunting him.

Approaching cautiously, Deven found himself face to face with the stranger. Her gaze held a mixture of surprise and intrigue, as if she had not expected to encounter anyone at the bungalow. Deven cleared his throat, the weight of his thoughts evident in his tone as he spoke, "Good afternoon. Can I help you with something?"

The elderly woman's eyes studied him for a moment before she finally spoke, her voice carrying a hint of hesitation. "I couldn't help but notice you coming out of this bungalow. Are you... are you the new owner?" Her words were tentative, and her curiosity was unmistakable.

Deven nodded, a sense of anticipation building within him. "Yes, I recently inherited this bungalow," he replied, his curiosity matching hers. "Did you know the previous owner, Mrs. Joshi?"

The woman's expression shifted, a subtle mix of emotions flickering across her features. "Ah, Mrs. Joshi..." she trailed off, her voice carrying a wistful note. "Yes, I knew her. We were neighbours for many years. My Husband was tax consultant for Mr.Alok Joshi . My Name is Mrs Chhaya Pathak.

Deven's heart quickened at the confirmation of his hunch. "Could you tell me about her? I've been trying to understand her story, but it's shrouded in mystery."

The woman's eyes seemed to gaze into the distance, lost in memories of times past. "Mrs. Joshi was a kind woman, quiet and reserved. She lived alone; you know. Her disappearance, it was quite sudden and left the neighbourhood in shock." Her voice held a touch of sadness, a hint of memories that held more than met the eye.

Deven felt a sense of urgency as he asked, "Do you know anything about why and how she disappeared, or any unusual occurrences in this bungalow?"

The woman's eyes met his, a flicker of something enigmatic passing through her gaze. "There were rumours, whispers among the neighbours," she began slowly. "Strange things happened here, things that no one could explain. As for Mrs. Joshi... well, some believed that she was haunted by her past, that there were secrets she couldn't escape."

Deven's heart raced, his curiosity and unease intertwining. The pieces of the puzzle were slowly falling into place, but the mystery was far from solved. The elderly woman seemed to hold a key—a connection to Mrs. Joshi and the secrets that had driven her to the shadows.

So, what was she like?" Deven's voice held an undercurrent of curiosity as he faced Mrs. Pathak, his gaze locked onto her with an intensity born of intrigue. "Why was she living alone in this bungalow all by herself?"

Mrs. Pathak's expression took on a thoughtful cast, as if she were sifting through memories long buried. Her eyes seemed to gaze into the past, searching for the right words to encapsulate the enigma that had been Mrs. Asha Joshi.

She was a woman of quiet elegance," Mrs. Pathak began, her voice carrying a reverent tone. "A presence that exuded a certain mystery, as if she carried the weight of untold stories within her. Mrs. Joshi was a very private person, we used to meet only for the kitty parties and bhajan sandhya which used to happen in the colony's Mandir, but there was always a certain distance about her—a sense that she held a world apart from the rest of us.

"And the bungalow?" Deven continued, his tone earnest. "Did anyone know about her disappearance?

Mrs. Pathak's expression turned solemn, the weight of history settling upon her features. "Her disappearance was as abrupt as her presence was enigmatic. One day, she was here, and the next, she was gone. No one could explain it. The doors were locked from the inside, but she had vanished without a trace.

"Asha managed this house on her own after losing her husband," Mrs. Pathak continued, her voice carrying a hint of admiration for the woman's strength."She handled everything-maintaining the bungalow, overseeing investments—it was as if she was determined to keep his legacy alive."

Deven's eyes widened in response, a newfound respect for Mrs. Joshi blossoming within him. The woman's determination to maintain the bungalow's legacy and her husband's memory despite her enigmatic nature spoke volumes about her character.

"And what happened to her husband?" Deven's question hung in the air, his curiosity piqued by the implication that there might be more to the story.

Mrs. Pathak's gaze met his with a mixture of surprise and realization. "You don't know?" Her voice held a trace of astonishment. "Asha's husband, Mr. Alok Joshi, disappeared in the same mysterious manner from this very house ten years ago"

Deven's eyes widened in shock, his mind racing to process the revelation. The coincidence was too uncanny to dismiss. The bungalow seemed to hold a dark secret, a history of disappearances that defied all logical explanation. He could hardly believe what he was hearing.

"You mean to say that both Mr. and Mrs. Joshi disappeared in the same way?" Deven's voice trembled with a mixture of disbelief and intrigue.

Mrs. Pathak nodded solemnly, her gaze never leaving his face. "Yes, it's as if this bungalow holds a secret that has claimed both of their fates. A secret that continues to elude us, even after all these years."

Deven's mind whirled, the weight of the revelation sinking in. The bungalow's history had taken on a chilling dimension, a web of mysteries that stretched back in time. He looked at Mrs. Pathak, his eyes reflecting the shock and uncertainty that had overtaken his thoughts.

As the truth settled upon them, Deven realized that the journey to uncover the bungalow's secrets had only just begun. The disappearance of both Mr. and Mrs. Joshi was a puzzle that demanded to be solved, a tale that held the key to the enigma that had become his obsession. With a sense of determination burning brighter than ever, he knew that he was committed to unravelling the truth, no matter how unsettling it might be.

"Okay Beta, I need to go, I will see you around, do come home sometime. I stay in the very next building; she pointed out her house from there and went away.

After Mrs. Pathak's departure, Deven found himself in the wake of conflicting emotions. A growing sense of duty tugged at his thoughts, urging him to delve further into the enigmatic tale of Mrs. Joshi. The encounter with the elderly woman had ignited a determination within him, a determination to uncover the truth that had remained hidden for so long. He stood at the entrance gate, contemplating the steps he needed to take next.

CHAPTER FOUR

Whispers in the Dark

After Mrs. Pathak's departure, Deven found himself in the wake of conflicting emotions. A growing sense of duty tugged at his thoughts, urging him to delve further into the enigmatic tale of Mrs. Joshi and Mr Joshi. The encounter with the elderly woman had ignited a determination within him, a determination to uncover the truth that had remained hidden for so long. He stood at the entrance gate, contemplating the steps he needed to take next.

The urgency to unearth the mysteries that had woven themselves around the upper floor surged within him. He thought of Mrs. Asha Joshi, a woman whose life had become a series of unanswered questions. Deven's resolve crystallized as he considered the possibility of finding a photograph, a visual link to the elusive figure who had inhabited the bungalow.

The courage he had summoned before, the same courage that had led him through the unsettling discoveries, now compelled him to reenter the bungalow. The familiarity of the rooms he had explored earlier was juxtaposed with the weight of the unknown, the history that beckoned him to uncover its secrets.

As he crossed the threshold once more, Deven felt a heightened awareness of the atmosphere around him. Every creak of the floorboards, every flicker of light, seemed to carry a whisper of the past. He navigated through the rooms with a purpose, guided by the determination to uncover more about Mrs. Joshi's presence in the bungalow.

The photographs that lined the walls captured his attention, each image a frozen fragment of time. Deven's eyes scanned the faces, searching for the visage of Mrs. Asha Joshi. The room's air seemed to thicken with the weight of expectation, as if the photographs themselves held the key to unravelling the mysteries that had eluded him.

With each step, Deven felt a renewed connection to the bungalow. The rooms that had once seemed empty were now charged with the promise of revelation.

Deven's footsteps echoed softly as he entered Mrs. Joshi's private space—the bedroom that had once been a haven of her secrets and solitude. The air in the room was charged with a sense of reverence and anticipation, as if the walls themselves held the echoes of her presence. With a mixture of trepidation and determination, he began his hasty search, his hands moving with a sense of urgency.

He scanned the room, his eyes darting from one corner to another, searching for any clue that could shed light on the mysterious woman's life. Drawers were opened and rifled through, their contents revealing fragments of her past—a collection of aged letters, a faded photograph, and trinkets that held sentimental value. Deven's heart raced, the weight of his mission propelling him forward. He knew he was grasping at straws, yet the compulsion to unearth a connection, to find a thread that could unravel the enigma, drove him forward.

Deven's gaze fell upon the shelf next to Mrs. Joshi's bed, his eyes locking onto an old, weathered photo album that seemed to beckon him. Deven's heart raced as he noticed the photo album resting just below the shelf, its presence seemingly waiting for him to discover. His fingers reached out instinctively, his anticipation growing with each passing second. As he opened the album, he was greeted by more images, each one a piece of the puzzle he was trying to decipher. With a mix of anticipation and curiosity, he reached for the album, his fingers brushing against the aged cover. He settled onto the edge of the bed, the creak of the mattress beneath him.

Opening the album revealed a world frozen in time, photographs capturing moments that spanned decades. Deven's heart quickened as he flipped through the pages, his eyes drinking in the sepia-toned images that told the story of Mrs. Joshi's life. There were candid snapshots of family gatherings, formal portraits of generations long past, and scenes of everyday life that offered glimpses into a bygone era. His fingers lingered on the last photograph in the album—a candid shot of Mr. and Mrs. Joshi, their expressions solemn and enigmatic, standing side by side in front of the bungalow. It was as if the photograph held a secret, a truth that had been concealed for decades.

His eyes lingered on a particular photograph, the one that had struck him as he flipped through the pages. Mrs. Asha Joshi, her radiant smile and youthful grace captured within the frame, stood beside her husband, Mr. Alok Joshi. The disparity in their appearances was undeniable. She appeared vibrant, her age seemingly defied by her beauty, while Mr. Alok Joshi was a study in contrast, his features marked by the passage of time. He considered the age gap he had discerned between them, the difference in their physical appearances, and the enigma of their relationship. Mrs. Asha Joshi's allure was undeniable, and the contrast with her husband's aging visage only accentuated her youthful charm. As Deven continued to flip through the photo album, his eyes widened in recognition as he came across a series of photographs that struck a chord of familiarity. The images were reminiscent of the photo frames he had stumbled upon earlier in the living area—the ones hanging on the walls of the bungalow. In these photographs, he recognized the same figures—Mrs. Shanti and Mr. Anand Joshi, Mrs. Asha Joshi's in-laws.

With every turn of a page, Deven found himself immersed in a different era, a different chapter of the bungalow's history. The photographs were more than mere visuals—they were windows to the past, offering a glimpse of the laughter, the tears, and the emotions that had once filled the rooms he now walked through.

But it wasn't just the album that caught his attention. Beneath it, he noticed a small bundle of red cloth—a potali—carefully placed. He lifted it gently, his curiosity piqued by the contents concealed within. As he unfolded the cloth, his eyes widened in surprise. Heart pounding with a mix of trepidation and exhilaration, Deven's hands moved with urgency as he untied the potali's knot. The red cloth fell away to reveal a small, weathered diary resting within, its now yellowed pages seemingly brimming with untold tales. The diary was a portal into her thoughts, her experiences, her emotions laid bare on paper. In one swift motion, he unlocked the diary's clasp and opened its pages. The first entry greeted him—an eloquent prose that bore the distinctive mark of Mrs. Asha Joshi's handwriting. As his eyes swept over the lines, a thrill coursed through him. It was as if Mrs. Joshi's voice was whispering across time, reaching out to him with an urgency that mirrored his own.

however, as the light outside began to dim, a jolt of realization surged through him. Hours had slipped away, the daylight making way for the encroaching shadows of evening. sense of urgency pierced through his fascination, and he tore his gaze away from the diary to cast a glance out the window. The sun's descent had painted the sky in hues of orange and pink, and darkness was gathering with every passing moment. A chill ran down his spine as he remembered the unsettling note he had discovered earlier—the note that had urged caution and warned him not to stay past dark.

With the diary clutched in his hand, he stood up from the bed, glancing around the room as if bidding farewell to the secrets it held. With one last glance around the room, Deven made his way out, the diary was tightly held in his hand—a testament to the journey he had undertaken, a journey that was far from over.

He came out from the main door.The bungalow's doors closed behind him, sealing away the stories within its walls. But as Deven stepped out into the fading daylight, he carried with him the weight of Mrs. Joshi's narrative and the promise of uncovering the truth that had remained hidden for so long.

As Deven locked the heavy wooden door behind him, a palpable sense of unease gripped his chest. The weight of the bungalow's mysteries still clung to him, like a lingering presence that refused to let go. He glanced around the dimly lit room one last time, shivers coursing down his spine as the air seemed to thicken with the weight of the unknown.

Summoning a semblance of normalcy, he picked his phone and called an Uber, his fingers tapping with an urgency that belied his attempt to appear composed. The minutes dragged by, each second feeling like an eternity as he stood outside the imposing gate, eyes flickering between the shadowy depths of the garden and the muted glow of his phone's screen.

Finally, the soft hum of an approaching engine broke the silence, and relief surged through him as the Uber came into view. The driver's friendly smile was a stark contrast to the lingering unease that had settled upon him like a shroud. Climbing into the cab, Deven exhaled a breath he hadn't realized he was holding, the desire to distance himself from the bungalow's unsettling aura overpowering all else.

As the car pulled away, he cast one last glance over his shoulder, his heart racing for reasons he couldn't quite fathom. The bungalow loomed in the distance; its dark silhouette etched against the fading evening sky. And then, as if in response to his gaze, something shifted within the darkness—a shadow that seemed to detach itself from the bungalow's façade.

Deven's breath caught in his throat as his eyes locked onto the figure, frozen in place by a mixture of fear and fascination. The shadowy shape appeared to be staring directly at him, its presence both ominous and intriguing. He could almost sense the weight of its gaze, a sensation that sent a shiver down his spine.

Just as quickly as it had appeared, the shadow vanished, melting back into the obscurity of the bungalow. Deven's heart raced, his mind racing to make sense of what he had just witnessed. Doubt gnawed at him, whispering that his imagination was playing tricks, but the chilling reality of the encounter refused to be dismissed.

As the cab carried him away from the bungalow, the unsettling image remained imprinted on his mind. He knew that he couldn't escape the bungalow's grip on his thoughts, and the lingering question—had he truly seen something beyond explanation—loomed like a specter, refusing to be banished by rationality.

CHAPTER FIVE

The Diary

Deven's mind was a whirlwind of confusion as he sat in the cab, the familiar chaos of Pune's traffic suddenly offering a strange comfort. The ordinary hustle and bustle of the city seemed like a shield against the enigmatic occurrences that had enveloped the bungalow. His thoughts raced, a tangled mess of fragmented experiences and unanswered questions that refused to be ignored.

The image of the shadow stared back at him, haunting his mind like a ghostly apparition that defied explanation. What had he truly seen? And were the handprints and footprints in the attic connected to the shadowy figure? The implications of the bungalow's secrets seemed to deepen with each passing moment, a puzzle with pieces that refused to fit together.

The coincidences were too eerie to ignore—the unexplained disappearances of both Mr. and Mrs. Joshi, the peculiar warning note that he had found in that very room, the unsettling experiences in the upper floor. As he reflected on these events, Deven felt as though he was being drawn into a labyrinth of mysteries, a web spun by the bungalow's history.

His determination to uncover the truth was matched only by his growing apprehension. The path ahead was fraught with uncertainty, and he couldn't shake the feeling that he was inextricably entwined in a narrative that spanned generations. The bungalow held the key, but deciphering its secrets seemed like an insurmountable task.

As the cab carried him closer to his home, Deven's mind remained locked in a battle between curiosity and caution. The bungalow's allure was undeniable, but the warnings and the eerie occurrences were impossible to ignore. His journey to solve the mystery was akin to navigating a treacherous maze—one that promised answers, yet threatened to ensnare him in a web of darkness.

With a sense of relief, Deven rushed into his apartment building. The familiarity of his own living space offered a sanctuary of sorts, a place where the shadows of mystery could be momentarily set aside. He stepped into the elevator and took a deep breath, the small space providing a sense of security as it carried him upward.

The realization struck him that he hadn't eaten anything the entire day. A wave of hunger surged through him, a reminder of his physical needs amidst the mental turmoil. He decided to order food online, opting for the convenience that modern technology offered. As he waited for his order to arrive, he sank onto his couch, the sense of normalcy gradually returning.

The aroma of the food filled his apartment as he devoured his meal, the physical nourishment easing the tension that had settled in his muscles. With his stomach full and the night deepening outside his window, Deven's thoughts turned back to the diary he had brought home from the bungalow—a relic that held the potential to unlock the mysteries that had consumed his mind.

The night outside grew darker, but within the walls of his apartment, a new journey was unfolding—one that would lead him closer to the truth, no matter how unsettling or unexpected it might be.

Deven sat on his couch, the diary resting in his hands like a treasure chest of secrets waiting to be unlocked. The pages held the promise of unravelling the mysteries that had haunted him, and with a sense of anticipation, he opened the diary. Mrs. Joshi's handwriting greeted his eyes—a graceful script that seemed to bear the weight of years gone by. Each curve and stroke told a story of its own, a testament to the woman who had penned these words.

As he turned to the first page, a picture of Lord Ganesha met his gaze, his benevolent presence casting a reassuring aura over the endeavour ahead. Above the image, a swastik drawn with kumkum added an air of sanctity, a silent affirmation of the significance of these written words. The initial lines were simple yet evocative, revealing the introspective nature of the woman who had penned them

I don't know what is happening around, I don't know if it is real, But I should now start writing it down. to keep a track of things happening around. to keep a track of things happening around. Perhaps I am caught in a web of hallucinations, much like my husband Alok,

When did this all truly begin? Was it in the wake of Alok's sudden and unexplained vanishing, leaving behind a void that haunts me to this day? Or does the thread of mystery stretch back even further, unraveling its enigma over the

span of decades? Perhaps it harks back to the time when my father-in-law, too, vanished from this very house, following the same inexplicable pattern. Or does it trace its origins even further, back to the disappearance of my own mother-in-law? The echoes of these inexplicable events resonate through the corridors of time, shrouding this house in an aura of intrigue and foreboding. As I put my thoughts to paper, I hope to piece together the puzzle that has gripped my life in a web of uncertainty and riddles.

Alok held a steadfast aversion to discussing these matters, a reluctance that extended to the very core of his being. An impenetrable wall surrounded the topic, shielding it from any probing inquiries. It was as though a storm brewed beneath his calm exterior, waiting to erupt whenever the disappearance of his parents was mentioned. Anger, raw and unyielding, would flash across his eyes, an emotion he struggled to contain. In the wake of his silence, I found myself adrift, yearning for answers that seemed forever out of reach.

Nearly six decades have passed within the embrace of these walls, and the memories of those days remain etched in my mind with vivid clarity. The year 1962 marked the beginning of a new chapter in my life, as I embarked on the journey of marriage with Alok. The house, once unfamiliar, soon became a canvas on which I painted the hues of my dreams and aspirations. As a young bride, I embraced each corner, each room, and wove threads of familiarity and comfort into every nook and cranny. I labored to infuse this house with the essence of our love, transforming it into a sanctuary where two souls intertwined and forged a life together. In those early days, amidst the laughter and the challenges, I found myself stitching together the tapestry of my existence, shaping this house into a cherished home that would cradle our shared memories and stories.

The memory of that first visit to this grand bungalow remains etched in my mind as though it happened just yesterday. The sheer scale of it left my father and me astonished; its opulence stood in stark contrast to the modest life we had known. From the humble abode that nestled behind the Shiv Mandir, where my father served as a pujari, we now stood before the grandeur of this house.

My roots were firmly anchored in the soil of a modest Brahmin family. The mandir's trust had provided us with a small room, a place that held only the most basic of amenities—a simple washroom and a small kitchen. Yet, it was within those four walls that I learned the sacred art of tending to the temple and aiding in the rituals. My days were spent in devotion, and the rhythm of the mandir's routines became my solace.

And then, as fate would have it, I was introduced to a life beyond the temple's boundaries. My father-in-law, along with my mother-in-law, often graced the temple with their presence. It was there that our paths converged. I believe my sincerity and skill in managing the intricate tasks of cooking, performing rituals, and overseeing the mandir's various functions caught her discerning eye. Her fondness for me, I believe, was rooted in my youth and, perhaps, the radiant charm I held back then.

The transition from the mandir's small quarters to this sprawling bungalow felt like stepping into a surreal realm. For someone who had cherished the simplicity of a life dedicated to the divine, the prospect of residing in this house was nothing short of a dream. The allure of the grandeur and the promise it held for a future I had never envisioned left me both exhilarated and apprehensive, as if I had crossed a threshold into a world that was both enchanting and unfamiliar.

"Please welcome Dixit Guruji", my father-in-law who were waiting for us welcomed me and my dad with a warm smile, as my father and I exchanged puzzled glances, it was evident that we were stepping into an occasion of significance, though the nature of its importance remained veiled. I speculated that it might pertain to a sacred ceremony, perhaps Satyanarayana pooja to sanctify their home. Little did I know that destiny had plotted a different course for that moment, one that would change the trajectory of our lives.

Seated together in the serene embrace of the garden that adorned the premises, my father appeared somewhat reserved. The air was thick with anticipation, the unspoken questions hanging in the midst of the gathering. Breaking the ice, my father, asked. "I still don't understand," addressing my father-in-law directly, "what prompted you to invite us here?

A soft smile played upon my father-in-law's lips, his eyes reflecting a blend of fondness and respect. With a calm demeanor, he responded, "We hold your daughter in high regard, and if you permit and if she agrees, I would like to ask for her hand for my son, Alok." His words hung in the air, weighted with the gravity of the proposal he had presented. My father-in-law's smile broadened, his pride and affection for Alok evident in his gaze. "Allow me to introduce my son, Alok," he added, as if presenting Alok through his words."

Alok, he explained, is a government bank clerk, his steady occupation promising security and stability. The mention of my father-in-law's own prominent role in the public welfare department hinted at a life well-established and connected. As the words flowed, I found myself engulfed in a mixture of emotions—surprise, gratitude, and a tinge of nervousness. It was an introduction not just to Alok, but also to the possibilities that lay ahead.

"We are a family that stands on firm ground," my father-in-law continued, his words carrying an air of reassurance. "We understand that this situation may seem awkward, even overwhelming, at this moment." His gaze softened as he looked towards me, a gesture that held a promise of understanding and patience.

He leaned forward, his expression kind and sincere. "Let me assure you," he said, his voice steady, "she will find happiness here." The weight of his assurance settled in the air, resonating with a sense of responsibility and care. "In this house, we have nurtured an environment that offers all that she could ever need," he affirmed. The reassurance he offered was more than just words; it was a pact forged in that very moment, a pact to safeguard the happiness and comfort of the woman who held the center of my being

"But, Dada," my father's response resonated with a tone of honesty and vulnerability, "I am but a humble pandit with limited means." His words carried the weight of his integrity, each syllable a reflection of the truth he sought to convey. "To marry her into a family of such stature," he continued, his voice soft but resolute, "would necessitate a sum that exceeds my financial capacity." His words were neither brash nor disrespectful; instead, they were imbued with a candidness that came from a place of love and concern.

In that moment, I felt a surge of respect for my father, for his unwavering commitment to his principles and his willingness to voice his concerns, even in the face of uncertainty. The sincerity of his words underscored the importance he placed on transparency and the well-being of his daughter—a sentiment that transcended the societal norms that often governed such conversations.

As he expressed his limitations, I sensed a genuine dialogue unfolding between two fathers, each with a shared concern for their children's happiness. My father-in-law's response, I hoped, would mirror the respect my father had shown, acknowledging his concerns while perhaps offering a perspective that extended beyond mere finances. In this interaction, a bridge was being built, connecting two families and setting the stage for a union that would shape the lives of generations to come.

My father-in-law's smile remained steady, a silent acknowledgment of my baba's honest expression. With a warmth that radiated acceptance, he spoke, "Guruji, please understand, my wife and I hold the utmost reverence for you. Our visits to the mandir have given us a profound sense of spirituality, one that we recognize as a sacred inheritance passed down through generations."

The sincerity of his words enveloped the space, resonating with a depth of appreciation that transcended mere words. "You need not harbour any concern about the expenses associated with the marriage," he assured, his tone gentle and reassuring. "In our eyes, the value of the gift you will be bestowing upon us is immeasurable." His words held a sentiment that went beyond financial considerations, expressing a profound understanding of the intangible qualities that truly mattered.

The exchange between the two fathers embodied a spirit of mutual respect, an understanding that the essence of their conversation extended beyond monetary matters. As my father-in-law articulated his thoughts, I recognized the genuine appreciation he held for the values my baba had instilled in me—a recognition that surpassed any material expectations. In that moment, it was evident that the forthcoming union was more than a transaction; it was a merging of legacies, a culmination of shared values, and a pledge to uphold the sanctity of love and family.

Amidst the dialogues that resonated in that moment, I became aware of Alok's gaze upon me. His eyes, like a silent conversation, seemed to hold a mixture of curiosity, anticipation, and perhaps a touch of nervousness. It was as if his gaze conveyed a unspoken invitation—a chance to unravel the layers that separated us and build a bridge between our worlds.

And then, in her soft and endearing voice, my mother-in-law, a beacon of kindness and understanding, addressed Alok. "Beta," she said with a gentle smile, "why don't you show her around the house? You can take this opportunity to ask her any questions you might have. I'm sure she, too, has her share of queries. Spend some time together, have a chat." Her words were more than just a suggestion; they were an affirmation of her compassion and empathy, a testament to her nurturing spirit.

In that instant, it felt as though a door had been opened—a door that led to a world awaiting exploration, a world of conversations, shared experiences, and perhaps the unveiling of unspoken aspirations. As Alok and I exchanged glances, a mutual understanding passed between us. With a nod, he gestured for me to join him, the unspoken invitation now made manifest in his actions. And so, with my heart both fluttering and resolute, I stepped forward, ready to embark on a journey that would bind our lives together in a tapestry of emotions, questions, and the promise of a shared future.

As Alok guided me through the house, a conversation that would shape the contours of our future unfolded. His words were both candid and thoughtful, carrying a weight that bespoke his genuine intentions. "Asha," he began, his tone a blend of sincerity and understanding, "I can imagine that all of this must be quite sudden for you. Your thoughts, your opinions—they matter greatly, and I want you to know that there is absolutely no pressure."

His reassurance hung in the air like a comforting embrace, a sentiment that dissolved any unease that might have lingered. He continued, his voice gentle but resolute, "My parents have spoken very highly of you. They admire the values you hold and the person you are. For me, it's important that my partner sees this family as her own, someone who respects the bonds we share." As he spoke, his gaze held mine, an unspoken invitation to share my thoughts openly.

In that moment, I felt a sense of respect and acknowledgment that touched my heart. Alok's approach was a far cry from the stereotypical notions that often-defined arranged marriages. It was a conversation marked by consideration, a mutual recognition of our individuality and autonomy. His words illuminated the path ahead, reminding me that this union was not about conforming, but about finding a shared ground where our aspirations and values could intertwine.

With a mixture of gratitude and vulnerability, I replied, "Alok, I must admit that all of this has taken me by surprise and left me feeling overwhelmed. However, when I consider the practical aspects, I realize that sooner or later, I will have to make this decision." have heard nothing but kind and respectful things about your family," I continued, acknowledging the reputation they held within our community. "Your parents, their values, and the warmth they have shown me—they all speak to the foundation of respect and understanding that I believe is essential in any relationship."

As we continued to explore the house, I sensed that the conversation had set a tone of open communication, one that would serve as the cornerstone of our shared journey, should we choose to embark upon it.

Amidst our conversation, a gentle interruption came in the form of Alok's mother calling us for tea. We made our way back to the garden, where the comfort of familiarity mingled with the unspoken dialogue that had been exchanged between us. As we settled down, the air held a sense of anticipation, a tangible reminder that this moment held the power to shape the course of our lives.

Seated once again in that tranquil space, Alok's father broached the question that hovered like a cloud over us: "So, what is your decision?" His words carried a blend of curiosity and respect, a recognition of the significance of the moment. It was a question that mirrored the swiftness with which life-altering decisions were often made in our society—an interplay of tradition and pragmatism that had long intrigued me.

As Alok's father's words hung in the air, Alok himself spoke up, his tone steady and resolute. "I am ready for this marriage," he said, his words carrying a note of earnestness that was both endearing and profound. "I've found a connection with her, and I genuinely like her. If Asha has no objections, I believe we can move forward with this." It was a gamble, as you aptly put it, a gamble where the stakes were nothing less than the course of our lives. And in that gamble, it seemed that the dice had rolled in our Favor, offering a promise of a shared future—a future built on communication, understanding, and a choice rooted in mutual respect.

As I glanced at my father, a mixture of emotions swirled within me. His eyes held a blend of pride, love, and a touch of emotion, all veiled beneath a veneer of understanding. I could almost read his thoughts, a father's heart bared for a moment—grateful for the alliance that had presented itself, overwhelmed with the journey his daughter was about to embark upon, and holding a silent affirmation for the path she was choosing.

In that moment, his subtle nod spoke volumes. It was an unspoken approval, a father's way of conveying that he entrusted this decision into my hands, believing in the choices I was making for my own happiness With a heart that was a mixture of excitement, uncertainty, and a dash of bashful delight, I found my voice. Head slightly bowed and hands gently folded, I expressed my sentiment with a smile that held a trace of shyness. "If this is the wish of all our elders," then I, too, have no objections in moving ahead with this alliance."

as our voices united in agreement, it felt as though the universe itself had conspired to bring us together, to shape our lives in a way that defied the boundaries of chance.

Within the span of a month, the threads of destiny wove a tapestry that led me to Shanti Villa, a place that had once seemed so distant, yet now held the promise of becoming my home. The whirlwind of preparations culminated in a wedding that embraced tradition, warmth, and the merging of two families into a singular bond.

True to his word, Alok's father orchestrated every detail with meticulous care. From the attire I adorned to the jewellery that I wore; every facet was taken care without burdening my father's and maintaining his dignity and grace. The air was filled with a vibrant blend of celebrations, and the villa transformed into a realm of festivity, its walls echoing with laughter, music, and the joy of union.

The presence of relatives from Alok's side was a testament to the close-knit fabric of their family. On my side, a more intimate circle graced the occasion. Among them, my mother's sister, and her daughter Usha, stood as a beacon of support and connection, a link to my past and a guide to the future. The mehndi adorned my hands, the haldi brought a glow to my skin, and the pheras bound us in a vow that transcended words. The wedding was more than an event; And as I stepped into this new phase of life, guided by tradition and buoyed by the spirit of family, I recognized that the decision I had made was a culmination of choices—my own, those of my parents, and the subtle hand of fate that had led me to this moment of togetherness.

Amidst the flurry of wedding preparations and celebrations, there was one detail that caught my attention—an aspect that seemed slightly unusual, yet was easily brushed aside amidst the excitement. Alok's father had chosen not to invite any of their relatives to stay at Shanti Villa during the wedding, despite the festivities being hosted within the very confines of the villa itself. Instead, a separate guest house had been arranged for their accommodation. The decision, though subtle, lingered in the back of my mind. It was an observation that, while puzzling, didn't immediately raise any red flags. The momentum of the occasion, the joyous atmosphere, and the anticipation of starting a new life overshadowed any lingering questions. I trusted in the arrangements made by Alok's father, and my focus remained fixed on the unity of our families and the beginning of our shared journey. Little did I know that it was a mere fragment of a larger puzzle, one that would later reveal itself as part of a tapestry interwoven with secrets and mysteries that were yet to unfold.

the echoes of wedding celebrations began to fade, a sense of tranquility settled over Shanti Villa. The grand festivities had concluded, and the villa's ornate halls now stood quiet As the guests departed, a hush enveloped the villa, and it was in this calm that the weight of change bore down on me. My father, a constant presence and pillar of support, stood before me with a mixture of pride and emotion. The realization that I would no longer be returning home with him tugged at my heart, and unspoken words lingered between us. In this tender juncture, Alok's father extended his assurance, his words a balm for the unspoken ache. "Guruji," he said, his voice carrying both reverence and warmth, "you are always welcome in this house. Consider it your own home, a place where you can find solace and companionship whenever you feel the need." His invitation was imbued with sincerity, a bridge that spanned the gap between my past and the life I was embarking upon.

With eyes brimming with unshed tears, my father left, his footsteps fading into the night. It was a moment of farewell and new beginnings, of embracing change while treasuring the bonds that shaped our existence. Left with the intimacy of the four of us, dinner was shared, although my appetite was subdued by the emotions that still lingered.

Finally, as the night's embrace grew, we headed to our bedroom. In the quietude, amidst the echoes of promises exchanged and rituals observed, the significance of the day enveloped us. As we settled into our new life, the vastness of the bungalow and the mystery that seemed to echo within its walls held the promise of a future intertwined with secrets, love, and the enigmatic tales of Shanti Villa.

Stepping into the expanse of our new bedroom, I felt a mixture of awe and gratitude wash over me. The room itself was larger than the tiny space that had been my home for years—a space that held memories of simplicity, of prayers and devotion whispered in quiet moments. Now, as I looked around at the grandeur of our bedroom, I realized how much my life had transformed.

The journey from that small room to this vast chamber was marked by twists of fate, by the twists and turns of destiny that had led me to this moment. As I gazed upon the lavishness around me, I acknowledged that it was never the wealth or riches that had drawn me, but the blessings of family, love, and the threads that had woven themselves into the fabric of my life.

So, as I settled into the soft embrace of our new bed, I closed my eyes with a heart filled with gratitude. The bunglow and its mysteries were now an integral part of my life, a place where secrets lay waiting to be unraveled. But amidst it all, the foundation that held me steady was the love and respect that defined the relationships I held dear. With that sense of gratitude, I drifted into dreams, knowing that whatever lay ahead, I was equipped with the most precious treasures of all—family, love, and the unfolding journey of life itself.

Within the span of a few days, the rhythm of Shanti Villa began to harmonize with my presence. I embraced the mantle of household chores, transitioning into the role of a wife and homemaker with a sense of eagerness and determination. Alok's mother, a nurturing and gentle soul, extended a kindness that filled a void in my heart that I hadn't even known existed. Her presence was like a warm embrace, a connection that bridged the gap between my past and my new life.

Her time was often dedicated to the sacred rituals of the pooja room, a space that seemed to radiate with a tranquil energy.

Our bond deepened as I took charge of the kitchen, experimenting with flavors and creating dishes that carried a blend of my roots and the new family I had become a part of.

Meanwhile, Alok's father and I shared a relationship that was characterized by a respectful distance. He was a man of stature and reputation, a fact that was evident in the steady stream of visitors who sought his guidance and counsel. The bunglow itself seemed to expand along with his influence, as the rooms and grandeur of our home grew to match the expanse of his accomplishments.

Gifts and tokens of respect arrived regularly, offerings from people who recognized the value of his wisdom and leadership. Amidst the steady flow of visitors and their appreciation, I observed him with a sense of admiration, a silent acknowledgement of the legacy he had built. Despite the apparent distance between us, I recognized the depth of his character, the embodiment of a man who had carved a path of significance in his time

As I came across the various dynamics of my new life, I found myself embedded within a tapestry of relationships—each unique, each contributing to the mosaic that shaped my days at Shanti Villa.

With the passage of time, the ebb and flow of life began to take its toll on Alok's father. His retirement marked a shift, a transition from the bustling world of visitors and professional esteem to the quiet confines of Shanti Villa. The reality of his post's significance became starkly apparent, and the absence of the constant stream of people seemed to echo the shifting tides of his life. Staying home, it seemed, presented its own set of challenges—a reality that he grappled with in his own way.

Amidst these fluctuations, a glimmer of joy and anticipation breathed new life into our home. The news of my pregnancy was met with an outpouring of happiness, rekindling the spark that had once illuminated our days. The excitement was palpable, reflected in Alok's father's eagerness as he took it upon himself to build a separate room for the soon-to-arrive addition to our family. It was a time of celebration, of dreams taking shape, and of hope that whispered promises of a future filled with the laughter and joy of a child.

Yet, as life often unfolds, even the brightest moments can be tempered by unexpected sorrows. A mere twelve weeks into the pregnancy, an excruciating pain roused me from sleep one fateful midnight. In those quiet hours, as the pain ebbed and flowed, I chose not to disturb the slumber of the household, waiting for the dawn that promised relief. Morning arrived, but with it came an unsettling feeling that something was amiss. Urgency propelled us to the doctor's office, where the truth slowly unraveled—a truth that shattered our hopes and dreams.

The doctor's diagnosis confirmed our deepest fears: we had lost our baby. The nursery, once a canvas of possibilities, was now closed forever by the weight of our grief. The house, which had seen the highs and lows of our journey, now stood as a solemn witness to our heartache. In the wake of this devastating loss, silence gripped Shanti Villa once again. The sounds of joy and laughter were replaced with the echo of emptiness, the vibrant colours fading into muted hues.

Healing from such a profound loss takes time—a time that stretched out as I navigated the labyrinth of grief. The pain of losing a child is a wound that seeps into every corner of the heart, leaving an ache that seems unending. But within the darkness, glimmers of strength began to emerge—strength drawn from the bonds of family, the solace of time, and the enduring love that surrounded me.

As I gradually found my way back to the light, I understood that the heartache would forever remain a part of me. And while the nursery remained closed, its doors held the memory of a love that had once bloomed and would forever be cherished.

wo years later, the winds of hope stirred once again as I found myself pregnant. The cautious optimism that accompanied this news was met with the whispers of aching memories, a reminder of the past losses that had etched their mark on our hearts. And tragically, history repeated itself—the pain, the heartache, and the grief returned, echoing the very same path we had walked before. It was as if fate had cast a shadow over our hopes, a shadow that we could not escape.

With each loss, the weight of our grief seemed to deepen, etching lines of sorrow on our souls. The pain was a familiar companion, an unwelcome guest that had taken residence within the corners of our lives. And as we faced the same devastation yet again, a new reality began to dawn upon us—one that spoke of acceptance, of learning to navigate a world where our dreams of parenthood would never come to fruition.

Doctors' warnings resonated with a somber truth: my health was at risk, and another pregnancy could be perilous. With heavy hearts, we recognized that the road we had envisioned would forever remain closed

The prospect of adopting a child emerged as a potential alternative, a path that could fill our home with the laughter and presence of a young life.However, our dreams of adoption faced a roadblock in the form of Alok's father, who was firmly against the idea. His stance was resolute, and as a family, we arrived at an acceptance—an acceptance that this chapter of our lives would be marked by the absence of children. While the pain of unfulfilled dreams lingered, it was accompanied by a sense of closure. We had weathered storms of loss, and the resilience that blossomed from the depths of our grief fortified our spirits.

As the years passed, the halls of Shanti Villa bore witness to our shared experiences, our joys, and our sorrows. While the laughter of children never resonated within its walls, the echoes of our love and our enduring unity filled the spaces. Our lives had taken an unexpected turn, and in that twist of fate, we discovered the strength to embrace what was, to find solace in each other, and to cherish the countless moments that defined our unique and unbreakable family.

Amidst the shadows of my own grief, my focus had been tightly fixated on the pain that consumed me. But as time wore on, a shift in my perspective brought to light a peculiar transformation in Alok's mother. Her demeanor underwent a subtle metamorphosis, as if she carried a weight that she was reluctant to share. There was an air of unease that cloaked her, a constant tension that seemed to cast a shadow over her once serene countenance.

The transformation was evident in her every gesture—her delicate movements now betrayed a nervous energy, and her laughter, once hearty and carefree, now seemed tinged with an underlying apprehension. It was as though an unseen specter had taken residence within her, casting an enigmatic veil over her disposition. Even the slightest of sounds seemed to startle her, leaving her perpetually on edge, her senses attuned to something that remained beyond the grasp of understanding.

There was a palpable restlessness in her gaze, a searching intensity that spoke of a quest for something intangible. Her eyes, once mirrors of warmth and kindness, now held a distant look—a look that hinted at secrets hidden in the recesses of her consciousness. I found myself observing her with a mixture of concern and curiosity, wondering what shadows danced behind those veiled eyes, what secrets whispered in the corners of her mind.

In those moments of silent observation, I couldn't help but wonder about the intricacies of her own journey—the burdens she carried, the memories she held, and the enigma that seemed to envelop her. As my awareness expanded beyond my own sorrow, I began to perceive the intricate web of emotions that connected us all, weaving a narrative that extended far beyond my own grief.

Alok's mother remained an enigma, a puzzle that beckoned to be solved—a puzzle that was intertwined with the very fabric of Shanti Villa's history. In my pursuit of understanding, I felt a gradual shift, a widening of the lens through which I viewed the world around me. And as I delved deeper into the tapestry of our lives, I became acutely aware that the bunglow held more than just physical spaces; it held the echoes of stories—both whispered and unspoken—that were waiting to be unravelled.

As days turned into weeks, Alok's mother's transformation continued to unfold, leaving a trail of changes that were impossible to ignore. Her once lively presence in the colony's gatherings dwindled, and the sound of her laughter seemed to fade into the background. The ornate gold jewellery that had once adorned her seemed to lose its allure, replaced by the simplicity of cotton sarees, a mangalsutra, and glass bangles—a stark departure from the woman I had come to know.

Her retreat from the social fabric of our lives was evident, and it was as if she had distanced herself from the world in her quest for answers. The temple, once a place of solace and devotion, became her refuge, a sanctuary where she sought solace from the unspoken burdens that weighed upon her heart. The chime of the temple bells became a comforting echo, a respite from the echoes of silence that filled the bunglow.

Observing her withdrawal, I was filled with a growing sense of responsibility—a responsibility not only for my own emotions but also for the well-being of this woman who had become a pillar of our household. Her change in behavior was as perplexing as it was painful, and I felt a deep yearning to bridge the gap that had formed between us. Her transformation seemed to signify a shift not only in her own life but also in the dynamic of our family—an evolution that demanded understanding and compassion.

As the days passed, I found my resolve strengthening. The gnawing curiosity about the cause of her altered demeanor pushed me to confront the situation head-on. The thought of the child we had lost loomed large, but a suspicion lingered—an inkling that there was more to her transformation than met the eye. With a heart heavy with concern, I decided to breach the unspoken barriers that had formed between us, to initiate a conversation that held the potential to unveil the truths she held.

Summoning my courage, I found myself standing before the temple's entrance, where Alok's mother sat in quiet contemplation. The flickering lamp cast a gentle glow upon her features, accentuating the lines that etched her face with experience. With a deep breath, I softly asked, "Ma, is there something that's troubling you? Your change in behavior—it worries me."

Her gaze, once distant, now met mine—a gaze that held a myriad of emotions. A mixture of surprise, vulnerability, and a hint of relief crossed her eyes as she paused, seemingly contemplating her response. And in that moment, the threads of our lives seemed to converge, setting the stage for a dialogue that had the potential to bridge the gap that had grown between us—an opportunity to share the burdens that had remained unspoken for far too long.

In that fleeting moment, our eyes held an unspoken understanding—a connection that transcended words. A veil of vulnerability had lifted from her face, revealing the weight she had carried in silence for so long. I could sense the turmoil that churned within her, the struggle to decide whether to unburden herself or continue to bear the weight alone. The silence between us was filled with unspoken truths, and it was as if time stood still, granting us a space to communicate without words. Her gaze was both a plea and a question, a silent invitation to breach the walls that had kept us apart. It was a vulnerable expression that seemed to say,

As I continued to meet her eyes, I wanted to assure her that I was there to listen—to provide a space of empathy and understanding. I wanted her to know that whatever burden she carried, she didn't have to carry it alone. The gravity of her expression wasn't lost on me, and I felt a sense of responsibility to hold that space for her, to offer the solace she seemed to be seeking.

Sitting by her side, I listened intently to Alok's mother as she began to share the weight that had burdened her for so long. Her voice was filled with a mixture of sadness and determination, and her words carried the weight of truth that she had held onto in silence.

"Beta Asha," she began, her voice quivering with emotion, "I find it difficult to find solace within these walls anymore. It's as if this place has become a vessel for the sorrows of countless souls, a repository for the cries of the helpless and downtrodden." Her gaze drifted, as if she could sense the echoes of those unheard voices that lingered in the very air around us.

She continued, her words gaining momentum, "My husband, Alok's father, he holds a prominent position in society—a position built on the foundation of a good reputation. But beneath that facade, I've sensed the shadows of compromise and corruption. The wealth, the jewelry, the grandeur of this house—it's all constructed on the ashes of dreams that were shattered, of hopes that were left unfulfilled."

Her eyes held mine, filled with a mixture of pain and resolution. "This wealth, this prosperity, I believe it's tainted by the pain of those whose lives were marred by injustice. And in my heart, I've always carried the weight of this truth, a truth that has only grown heavier with time."

Alok's mother took a deep breath, her voice steadying as she confessed the most painful aspect of her reality. "And then there's the matter of our inability to have a child, to carry forward our lineage. I've often questioned why our home, which brims with material abundance, is devoid of the laughter and innocence of a child's presence."

Tears welled up in her eyes, and her voice trembled as she concluded, "I've come to believe that it's the weight of our karma, the karma that was shaped by the choices we've made, by the actions that have led to the suppression of others' dreams. This curse, this burden, I fear it's a consequence of the choices we've made."

As her words hung in the air, a heavy silence enveloped us—a silence that seemed to resonate with the echoes of her confession. In that moment, I realized that her journey wasn't just one of personal pain, but a shared realization of the price that had been paid for the riches and reputation that surrounded us. The conversation had lifted a veil, uncovering a truth that was both painful and transformative—a truth that had the potential to reshape the very fabric of our lives and our relationship with Shanti Villa.

With a deep sigh, she continued, "I had to withdraw from those colony ladies' gatherings. The talks, the whispers about Alok's father's reputation—they are like poison that seep into the corners of our lives. I couldn't bear the judgment, the questioning looks, the unspoken accusations. It's as if the walls of this house, the same walls that once felt like a haven, now hold echoes of those harsh opinions." "And then there are the nights," she confessed softly, "I find myself in a strange, unsettling dream. It's as if my consciousness is pulled away, and I'm wandering through the upper floors, through the attic. But it's not me—it's as if something else is moving me. And in that dream-like state, I feel a presence, a cry for help that echoes in my mind. It's haunting, Asha, and it leaves me feeling like I'm losing grip on reality."

As Alok's mother shared her innermost thoughts and feelings, I remained fully present, giving her my undivided attention. I could sense the weight of her words, the emotions that had been held back for so long, and the relief that came with finally letting them out. It was clear that she wasn't seeking immediate solutions or answers; she needed someone who would truly listen, someone who would empathize with her struggles without judgment.

Throughout her heartfelt confession, I offered my support in the form of a gentle touch, a comforting presence that conveyed my understanding and willingness to be there for her. As she spoke, I nodded in affirmation, acknowledging her pain, her fears, and the tangled web of emotions she had been navigating.

Sometimes, the most powerful thing we can offer is a listening ear—a safe space where our words won't be met with judgment or hurried solutions. Alok's mother had opened up a door into her inner world, and I was grateful to be entrusted with her thoughts. In that moment, our shared connection deepened, as did my resolve to stand by her side as we ventured into the unknown territory of Shanti Villa's mysteries.

and as we were talking the conversation suddenly got interrupted by a phone call on our land line.

"Hello?" I answered the phone.

"Hello?" I answered the phone, my voice laced with curiosity.

"Is it Mrs. Joshi?" the voice on the other end inquired. "I am calling from J J Hospital. Your father, Mr. Dixit, has been admitted here."

My heart skipped a beat as a surge of worry swept over me. "Yes, this is Mrs. Joshi. What happened to my father?"

"He was brought in a little while ago. We need you to come to the hospital as soon as possible," the voice replied with a note of urgency.

I didn't waste a moment. After thanking the caller, I hung up and immediately dialed Alok's number. As soon as he answered, I relayed the news. "Alok, we need to go to J J Hospital. Something's happened to my father, and they want us there."

Alok's voice was filled with concern. "Don't worry, Asha. Let's go there right away. We'll find out what's going on."

We both hurriedly left the house, our minds racing with worry and uncertainty. The mysteries of Shanti Villa seemed distant in that moment, replaced by the immediate concern for my father's well-being.

As we arrived at the hospital, the doctor met us to explain the situation. "Your father had a fall while doing household chores," he began. "He slipped and broke his left arm. We've taken X-rays and are assessing the extent of the injury."

As the doctor detailed what had happened, a rush of emotions swept over me. Seeing my father lying on the hospital bed, his usually strong and capable demeanor now replaced by vulnerability, a pang of guilt and sadness filled my heart. It struck me that this elderly man had been silently managing his struggles, not wanting to burden us with his challenges. My eyes welled up with tears as I realized how much he had endured on his own.

As Alok and I stood by my father's side, I couldn't help but feel a deep sense of regret that I hadn't been more attentive to his needs. In that moment, I resolved to be more present in his life, to offer him the same support and care that he had always provided me.

Two days later, as my father was about to be discharged from the hospital, a heartwarming moment unfolded that I hadn't expected. Alok, showing a depth of understanding and compassion that touched me deeply, sat next to my father and spoke with genuine care.

"Baba," he began, "we are aware of the traditional beliefs in our community, but I want you to know that our family doesn't hold such notions. At your age, it's important to have support and care. We would like you to come and stay with us, at least until your fracture is fully recovered. Please consider it."

I watched this exchange with a mixture of surprise and gratitude. Alok had not only recognized my father's need for assistance but had also acknowledged the potential hesitation that cultural norms might bring. His words resonated deeply, showing a level of consideration and empathy that went beyond societal expectations.

In that moment, my respect and admiration for Alok grew even strong.

My father hesitated, his concern for societal perceptions evident in his words. "Beta, how can I come over like this? What will people say?"

Alok's response was gentle yet firm, dispelling any doubts. "Baba, nobody will say anything. You need to come with us. Till date, I I haven't asked anything from you, but today I am being stubborn about this."

My father's reluctance melted away in the face of Alok's genuine concern and insistence. As we started on our journey back to Shanti Villa, a sense of uncertainty lingered within me. How would Alok's parents react to my father's presence in our home? What would they think of this sudden change?

To my surprise and relief, both of them welcomed my father with open arms and warm smiles. Alok's father spoke with kindness in his voice. "Guruji, no need to feel odd. This is your home as well. In fact, we regret not being here when you needed us during your emergency. Please don't feel awkward."

His words reassured not just my father, but all of us. It was heartening to witness the genuine hospitality and warmth extended to my father, erasing any doubts that might have lingered.

The positive change in Alok's mother's behavior was palpable. Her demeanor had transformed from one of tension and unease to that of happiness and contentment. She seemed genuinely pleased by my father's presence in our home, as if his arrival had lifted a weight off her shoulders.

One day, she approached my father with a request that pleasantly surprised us all. "Guruji," she said with a smile, "could you please perform the pooja at our mandir?" My father's eyes lit up, and he graciously accepted her request. It was heartwarming to see the bond between them strengthen through shared moments of spirituality and worship.

As my father immersed himself in the daily rituals, his harmonious presence seemed to infuse a sense of tranquility throughout Shanti Villa. The sense of mystery that once surrounded the house was slowly being replaced by a newfound unity and understanding among us all.

As we worked together in the kitchen one afternoon, Alok's mother spoke to me in a calm and serene tone. "Beta Asha," she began, "I feel so much at peace now. All those illusions I saw, the constant fear I experienced, they've all disappeared. Your father is a truly sacred soul. His presence has driven away whatever darkness once lingered here. He has brought life back to this house."

Her words filled the air with a sense of relief and hope. It seemed that my father's mere presence had dispelled the shadows that had haunted her for so long. She continued, her voice carrying a note of anticipation, "I am thinking of asking your father to stay here permanently. Alok's father will be delighted too, as he'll have a companion for his morning walks and tea."

Her suggestion brought a smile to my face. The idea of my father staying here permanently not only lifted her spirits but also promised a harmonious and joyful atmosphere in Shanti Villa. It was as if the power of my father's aura had cleansed the house, breathing new life into its walls and hearts.

My father had settled into a room adjacent to the nursery, which had remained closed for nearly five years. With his presence, more than two weeks had passed, and Shanti Villa's atmosphere had truly transformed. His arrival seemed to have brought a renewed sense of positivity that permeated the entire house. My father was a man of humility, even though he was now residing with us. He valued his financial independence greatly; in that era, living at his daughter's house was indeed a challenge to his sense of self-respect. As time went by, my father began to find his own ways of contributing to the household. He started bringing vegetables from the market and taking on his share of chores around the house. These small gestures not only helped him maintain his sense of independence but also added to the overall harmony of the household. Seeing him engaged and content brought joy to all of us.

After a month had passed, an eerie morning descended upon us. The clock struck 8 AM, and we were all gathered at the breakfast table, anxiously waiting for my father's presence. His routine was well-known – he would wake up at 5 AM, perform his morning pooja at our Mandir, accompany Alok's father for a walk, and return with fresh vegetables from the market. But on this particular day, something felt off. Alok's father decided to let him sleep in, not wanting to disturb his rest.

As the minutes ticked by, a growing sense of unease gnawed at me. Unable to ignore the feeling any longer, I ascended the staircase to call my father down for tea and breakfast. Upon reaching his room, a sight that would haunt me forever met my eyes. He was seated in an armchair, his pooja book clutched tightly in his hand. His eyes were wide open, an expression of terror etched on his face as if he had just witnessed something unimaginable. In a desperate gesture, he seemed to have reached out to his pooja book for protection or help.

The shock of what I saw overwhelmed me, and a scream involuntarily erupted from my lips. The shockwave rippled through me, and I collapsed, consciousness slipping away in the face of such inexplicable horror.

The doctor arrived, With a heavy heart, he declared that my father had passed away due to a heart attack. The words hit me like a tidal wave, and the world around me seemed to blur into a haze of disbelief. My mind struggled to process the reality – the one person who had been my constant source of support and love, who had sacrificed so much for me, was now gone.

Tears welled up in my eyes as the weight of the loss settled in. He had remained unmarried, devoted his life to me, and now I would never be able to see his smiling face again, to hear his reassuring words, to seek his guidance. The house that had felt like a sacred paradise was now a void, echoing with his absence. The realization that he was no longer there to share my joys and sorrows left an emptiness that words could not describe.

In the midst of the heart-wrenching grief, Alok and his father stood by me, offering unwavering support. They ensured that all the necessary rituals and ceremonies were conducted with the utmost respect and dignity. Alok, who had become not just my husband but a pillar of strength, took charge of the responsibilities that came with the situation. Together with his father, they performed the final rites, offering my father's mortal remains to the sacred flames.

Their presence during those trying times provided a sense of solace amidst the overwhelming sorrow. Alok's father's wisdom and guidance were invaluable, and Alok's unwavering support gave me the courage to face the reality of my father's absence. Even in my darkest moments, they stood by me, helping me navigate the painful process of bidding farewell to the person who had been my rock for so many years.

The passing of my father took a toll on Shanti devi, Alok's mother, in an unexpected way. Instead of finding solace in each other's grief, she seemed to be deeply affected by his departure, plunging into a state of emotional turmoil. It was as if the brief respite from her anxieties that my father's presence had provided had been abruptly shattered, and the fears and stresses that had haunted her returned with even greater intensity.

Her demeanour shifted, and the warmth that had characterized our relationship seemed to wane. She retreated into her own thoughts, appearing distant and detached when I expected her to provide comfort and support. I wondered if her connection with my father's presence was deeper than I had ever realized, or if there was something else at play that was triggering her distress. Her condition worsened, and I could sense that she was grappling with some internal struggle that was difficult to comprehend.

The dynamics of the house were shifting again, this time marked by a palpable unease and tension that hung in the air. As we navigated through this period of grief, uncertainty, and unresolved mysteries, the house itself seemed to hold secrets that were yet to be uncovered.

I looked at Alok's Mother with concern, my heart aching to understand the turmoil she was going through. Her eyes held a mixture of fear, vulnerability, and a sense of resignation. It was as if she had given up hope, as if some invisible weight was pressing down on her, rendering her unable to find solace or even articulate her emotions.

With a heavy sigh, she finally spoke, her voice wavering with a hint of desperation. "Asha, my dear, I can't explain it fully. It's like a cloud of darkness has settled over me. The fear, the anxiety—it's all too overwhelming. Your father's presence seemed to dispel it for a while, but now that he's gone, it's back. I can't escape it, no matter how hard I try."

Tears welled up in her eyes as she continued, "I feel like there's something in this house, something that doesn't want to let go. It's been here since Alok's father acquired this land by other means, which were not ethical, haunting us, taking away our happiness. I've tried to fight it, but it's like an invisible force that's beyond my control."

Her words sent shivers down my spine, as if confirming the unsettling feelings, I had experienced in this house. There was an eerie atmosphere, an unexplainable energy that seemed to linger in the air, influencing those who lived within its walls. Shanti devi's words painted a picture of a presence that was insidious, an entity that had woven itself into the very fabric of the house and the lives of its inhabitants.

As I listened to her, I realized that the mystery of this house ran deeper than I had ever imagined. The tales of disappearances, the strange occurrences, and now Shanti devi's own fears—all seemed to be interconnected in ways that defied logic and reason. I knew that uncovering the truth meant confronting whatever darkness was hidden within these walls, even if it meant confronting my own fears in the process.

Alok's mother looked at me, her eyes searching for solace and understanding. I could see the struggle within her, torn between the fear that gripped her and the hope I was trying to offer. She nodded slowly, her expression a mix of gratitude and uncertainty.

"Ma," I said gently, trying to comfort Shanti devi, "I understand that you're going through a difficult time, and it's natural for your mind to be overwhelmed by thoughts. But remember, we've faced several losses recently, and our minds can become fragile under such circumstances. It's easy for fear and negativity to take hold. You're not alone in this, and together we can find a way to overcome it."

I placed a reassuring hand on her shoulder, trying to convey my support and understanding. "Let's not let our minds wander into dark places. Instead, let's focus on the positive moments we've shared, the love that binds us as a family, and the memories we hold dear. The power of our thoughts can shape our reality, so let's choose to fill our minds with hope, strength, and the belief that things will get better."

Shanti devi looked at me, her eyes reflecting a mix of gratitude and uncertainty. It was clear that her fears were deeply ingrained, but I hoped that my words would offer her a glimmer of comfort. I wanted her to know that she wasn't alone, that we would face this challenge together and find a way to restore the sense of peace that had once graced our home.

As we sat there, hand in hand, I realized that our bond had grown stronger in the face of uncertainty. The shadows of the past were indeed haunting, but I was determined to shed light on the truth and bring peace to this house, for Shanti devi, for myself, and for all those who had lived within these walls, their stories waiting to be uncovered.

Over the next few days, I continued to closely observe Alok's Mother. Unfortunately, her condition didn't show any signs of improvement. It was disheartening to witness her struggle with her fears, and it became increasingly evident that something was deeply troubling her. What was even more puzzling was the fact that Alok's father seemed to maintain a distance from her, almost as if he was avoiding her emotional turmoil.

Her fear seemed to intensify with time. She would often be caught in a trance-like state, her gaze fixed on the staircase leading to the upper floor. It was as though that area held some sort of haunting presence that only she could perceive. Eventually, she stopped visiting the upper floor altogether, as if it held a dark secret that was too terrifying to confront.

One evening, Alok and I were attending a small gathering at his colleague's house. Alok's father had gone out for his regular evening walk and was planning to spend time at the senior citizen club in the nearby library, as was his routine.

When we returned home and opened the gate, Ma, came rushing toward us in a state of absolute terror. Her eyes were wide with fear, and she was almost breathless from panic. It took us nearly 15 minutes of reassurance and comforting words to calm her down.

As we tried to soothe her, I couldn't shake the feeling that something truly horrifying has been experienced by her.

We brought her inside and offered her a comforting cup of coffee. After a moment of calm, we gently asked her, "Ma, what has happened? Why are you so scared?" She took a deep breath and looked at us, her eyes still holding traces of fear. After a long pause, she began to speak.

"I was downstairs, sitting in the living room and watching the news on television," she started, her voice quivering. "And then suddenly, I heard a knock. It came from upstairs. For a moment, I thought it might be Alok's father returning from his walk and heading up to the rooms. I didn't pay much attention, as the TV was on and I was engrossed in the news."

She took another sip of her coffee and continued, "But then I heard it again, a thud. Like someone was moving quickly upstairs. That was strange because Alok's father would usually make his way quietly. I waited, expecting him to come down, but he didn't. Then, there was another sound, like someone running, but the footsteps were different, not like his."

Her voice trembled as she relived the experience, "As I sat there, the sounds seemed to grow louder, more pronounced. It was as if something was being dragged across the floor above, and the soft thuds turned into something more ominous. I felt a sense of unease, as if the sounds were approaching the ceiling and about to break through."

"I couldn't bear it any longer," she continued, her voice shaking, "I felt a rush of fear, and without thinking, I left the house and ran outside. I was terrified, and I could only find

solace when I saw you and Alok returning."

Listening to her account, a chilling realization washed over me. There was something deeply unsettling about the upper floor and the attic of the house, something that couldn't be explained by mere rationality. As I exchanged a concerned glance with Alok, I knew that we had to uncover the truth behind the enigma that had been haunting Shanti Villa for so long.

As we narrated Shanti devi's terrifying experience to Alok's father, he responded with a casual dismissal. "She has a habit of overthinking," he said with a calm tone, "It was windy today, and the iron shed on the roof might have had a few loose screws. It's probably just that sound. And we do need to get pest control done on the upper floor, there seem to be too many rats."

Alok's father's words seemed to downplay the intensity of Shanti devi's experience, attributing it to logical explanations. But the tension in the room was palpable, and the sense of unease couldn't be easily brushed aside. When Shanti devi heard his response, a wave of anger and frustration overtook her.

"Stop this madness now," she said, her voice wavering with both anger and fear. "This way, it will be difficult for us to show our faces in public. You can't keep ignoring what's happening here. There's something more to it, something we can't explain away with mere excuses."

As Shanti devi's words hung in the air, there was a distinct feeling that a veil of denial was slowly lifting, revealing the deeper undercurrents of mystery and unease that had plagued Shanti Villa for years. Despite Alok's father's attempts to rationalize the events, the unsettling experiences and the growing sense of dread couldn't be easily dismissed. The time had come to confront the unexplainable, to delve into the shadows and uncover the secrets that had been lurking within the walls of Shanti Villa for generations.

As the night stretched on, I found sleep elusive. My concerns for Alok's mother had intensified, and the events of the previous day replayed in my mind like a relentless loop. The growing unease and uncertainty were becoming difficult to ignore. I approached Alok, hoping to discuss the possibility of seeking medical assistance for his mother, but his response was a mixture of frustration and disregard. The matter seemed to close there.

When morning arrived, I felt a sense of urgency to check on Alok's mother. As I entered the kitchen, Lakshmi, our maid, had already arrived. I requested her to start chopping vegetables and fruits for breakfast while I started making tea. The usual routine involved Alok's mother joining me in the kitchen for tea at this time. However, with the tranquilizer she had taken the previous day, I guessed she might still be asleep.

Then, just as I was engrossed in my thoughts, I noticed Alok's father returning from his morning walk. The tense atmosphere from the previous day still lingered, and the unease in the house felt almost palpable. As he approached, I wondered if he had sensed it too, if he felt the weight of the mysterious occurrences that seemed to be closing in around us. The air was thick with unspoken words and hidden fears, and the day ahead promised to hold more questions than answers.

Me: Dada, would you like some tea? Also, is Ma still asleep?

Alok's Father: (Giving a strange look) What do you mean? She's not in the kitchen with you? When I woke up this morning, she wasn't in our room. I assumed she might be in the garden picking flowers for pooja or in the kitchen with you.

My heart skipped a beat at his response. The conversation took a sudden turn, and alarm bells started ringing in my mind. All of a sudden, a wave of worry for Ma washed over me.

I hurried into our bedroom to wake up Alok. We both started searching for Ma. Dada and Alok began their search outside, while I ventured inside the house. First, I checked the ground floor thoroughly, but there were no traces of her. Feeling increasingly concerned, I decided to call Laxmi, our house help, to accompany me in the search. Our house had four bedrooms on the ground floor, where the four of us usually stayed. The upper floor, which housed the library and Alok's father's collection of antiques, was rarely used due to the difficulty Ma and Dada had in climbing stairs.

As I gathered my courage to ascend the stairs, yesterday's incident vividly replayed in my mind. My legs were trembling, and my throat felt parched, but with Laxmi by my side, I managed to maintain some composure. We methodically searched every room on the upper floor. I even opened the nursery, which had remained untouched for a long time. Finding it empty eased my worries a bit. However, the inevitable moment arrived when I had to confront the attic. I couldn't recall when I had last been there, just standing at the door and quickly retreating due to the unsettling thoughts it stirred within me.

As I began descending the stairs, both Alok and his father were watching me with anticipation. I could sense their hopes were high. Sadly, all I could do was shake my head, and their expressions shifted to disappointment.

We all gathered in the dining room, the weight of the situation pressing heavily on us. Alok's gaze turned to me, his eyes reflecting regret, and he admitted, "I should have listened to you. She needed medical attention; her condition wasn't good yesterday." Alok's father shared his sadness and worry, expressing, "For so many days, she kept telling me to leave this house and shift somewhere else. I don't know what she was thinking. I've invested everything to build this house."

Taking a moment to reflect, I shared, "Dada, Ma wasn't in a good state of mind. She mentioned feeling someone's presence in the house, having hallucinations. Perhaps we should have paid more attention to it." Alok, his agitation palpable, quickly responded, "What are we discussing here? Ma is missing. We need to search for her." He turned to me, "Asha, please call her friends from her kitty group. Meanwhile, Dada and I will search nearby temples and hospitals. We don't know if she met with an accident or got disoriented after what happened yesterday. "His words resonated with practicality and urgency, making it clear that taking action was the most important thing at that moment.

the entire day passed in a state of anxious waiting, and despite our efforts, we couldn't locate her. Eventually, Alok decided to go to the police station to report her disappearance. They filed a missing person's complaint, and officers came to our house to conduct a search for any potential clues. They questioned our gardener about whether he had seen her leaving early in the morning, but he had no information. The watchman of the colony was also interviewed, and he confirmed that he hadn't seen anyone leave during the night or early morning.

Then, a question arose that none of us had thought of before. The watchman asked Alok's father, who was the first one to wake up and go out that day, if the front door was open when he left. Alok's father seemed taken aback by the question and replied, "I opened the door in the morning to go out, but it was locked." The realization hit us all – if the door was locked from the inside, it suggested that Ma had not left the house on her own accord.

The revelation that the front door was locked from the inside raised a perplexing question – if Ma hadn't left the house, where could she have possibly gone? The very thought sent shivers down our spines, and a sense of unease began to engulf us. We were faced with an unsettling mystery that defied logical explanation.

Despite the efforts of the police, days turned into weeks, and there was still no sign of Ma. Her photograph was published in newspapers, and Alok's father even offered a reward for any information leading to her whereabouts. But as time passed, hope began to wane. It was a heart-wrenching realization that she might never return. The silence that now hung over Shanti Villa was haunting, filled with unanswered questions and an eerie emptiness that seemed to echo the enigma that had engulfed her disappearance.

The void left by Ma's absence was palpable, affecting everyone in its own way. The house that once bustled with life and laughter now echoed with a haunting silence. Visitors and sympathizers came and went, leaving behind a trail of condolences and opinions. Some shared their sympathies, while others whispered about karma and destiny. But gradually, even the visitors began to dwindle, and Shanti Villa seemed to retreat into a melancholic solitude. Alok's father, who had always been accustomed to her presence, now found himself grappling with an overwhelming loneliness that he had never anticipated. The realization that she was no longer there, and the prospect of facing life without her, became an unimaginable pain he had to bear.

Alok's father's dependency on Ma had been so profound that he struggled to navigate even the simplest aspects of daily life on his own. As he grappled with this newfound solitude,

I did my best to assist him, stepping in wherever possible to help with his routine and provide companionship. However, I was surprised and disappointed by Alok's distant demeanor towards his father. Instead of offering emotional support, Alok seemed to maintain a noticeable distance, leaving his father to cope with his grief and loneliness largely on his own. It was disheartening to see their relationship strained during such a vulnerable time.

Alok's life had been considerably shaped by his father's influence, though often in subtle and indirect ways. Over the span of three decades, Alok refrained from seeking promotions within his government job. His father's words lingered in his ears – the notion that pursuing promotions would entail relocations to different cities, an idea his father didn't endorse. In those moments, his father would assert, "You don't need to work; we have sufficient savings. The money you earn is not my concern." Despite the financial independence Alok enjoyed, it was clear that his father's expectations and views about their family's togetherness held sway over his decisions. This dynamic might have contributed to Alok's perception of his father's role in his career trajectory and perhaps explained his average professional path.

As the days wore on, a shadow of decline descended upon Alok's father, casting a pall over Shanti Villa. Once a pillar of strength, his vitality now seemed to wither away. The simplest tasks became Herculean struggles, and his once sharp mind began to blur at the edges. The home that had once resonated with his authoritative presence now echoed with his confusion. Alok and I watched helplessly as he wandered through the house, lost in his own thoughts. Rituals and routines he once dismissed now became a refuge for him. The mandir, once visited occasionally, now became his sanctuary, a place where he sought solace and connection to something beyond the grasp of his failing memory.

Alok, increasingly concerned, sought medical advice, and the diagnosis was devastating: dementia, a thief that stole his memories and coherence. His once meticulous routines crumbled, replaced by fragmented actions and erratic behavior. The loss he had experienced and the weight of the years had converged, and he now grappled with this insidious ailment. A man who had always commanded respect and led by example was now slipping through the cracks of his own mind. The meals he once savoured became mere morsels, and I found myself coaxing him to eat like a parent urging a child. He withdrew from the world outside, abandoning his cherished senior citizen gatherings and abandoning his daily walks. Witnessing this once-strong figure fade into the haze of dementia was heart-wrenching, and the walls of Shanti Villa seemed to hold not just the echoes of its past, but also the poignant testimony of its present struggles.

In the midst of the ebb and flow of life's uncertainties, a year and a half after the unsettling disappearance of Alok's mother, a new chapter of unpredictability began to unfold. The air around Shanti Villa seemed to hold a mixture of unease and anticipation, as if the walls themselves were bracing for what was to come. Alok's father, who had been a silent observer of the shifting dynamics, began to display signs of restlessness, his normally taciturn demeanor now punctuated with sporadic outbursts of emotion. It was as though the weight of unspoken grief and unanswered questions was becoming unbearable for him.

Alok and I exchanged worried glances as we observed this transformation. The man who had always maintained a stoic facade was now revealing cracks in his emotional armor. Alok's attempts to engage his father in conversation were met with resistance, the older man deflecting questions and retreating into his thoughts. There were moments when his eyes held a distant sadness, a window into a world we couldn't fathom. It was clear that he was grappling with his own demons, but he seemed determined to keep them shrouded in secrecy.

The mystery of his internal struggles deepened as days turned into weeks. Alok made countless efforts to bridge the emotional chasm that seemed to have grown between father and son, yet each attempt was met with a stubborn silence. Shanti Villa, once a place of shared laughter and familial bonds, now held an undercurrent of tension, as if the house itself was privy to the silent battles being fought within its walls.

Just when we thought the currents of uncertainty couldn't grow stronger, another unexpected event rippled through our lives like a stone cast into a still pond.

Alok's father had disappeared, the same mysterious way Alok's Mother had disappeared.

The morning sun filtered through the curtains, casting a warm glow across the room. As I woke up, a sense of calm enveloped me, and I went about my morning routine. Alok was still asleep, lost in the embrace of slumber. It was a day like any other, or so I thought.

The doorbell's chime broke the tranquility, and I hurriedly made my way to the front door. Laxmi, our dependable house help, stood there, ready to start the day's chores. I requested her to make tea while I headed to the mandir, an integral part of our daily ritual.

However, this ordinary morning was marked by an absence that sent ripples of unease through me. Alok's father, the steady presence that had defined our mornings for so long, was nowhere to be seen. His routine of waking early, visiting the mandir, and performing his daily rituals was as predictable as the sunrise. Yet, on this day, he was conspicuously absent.

My concern deepened as I retraced his steps. His absence in the mandir was puzzling, and an anxious knot tightened in my stomach. The room that had once been filled with his quiet devotion now felt strangely empty. I crossed into his bedroom, hoping to find him there, perhaps resting a bit longer than usual. But the room was empty, his absence echoing in the air.

My worry intensified as I urged Laxmi to search the garden, hoping to catch sight of him amid the blossoming flowers. Her return, her expression grave, confirmed my fears—there was no sign of him. Panic began to set in, the tendrils of anxiety snaking their way into my thoughts.

I knew it was time to wake Alok, to share the disquiet that was now gripping me tightly. His slumber-laden eyes met mine, and I struggled to convey the sense of urgency that had taken over. The ordinary morning had unraveled into an unsettling mystery, the absence of Alok's father casting a shadow that seemed to stretch far beyond the bounds of our home.

As the minutes ticked by, my heart raced with worry, the unanswered questions becoming a weight that pressed heavily upon us. The once-familiar routine had been disrupted, and the reality of his absence hung over us like a cloud, shrouding our once-peaceful home in a veil of uncertainty.

We searched every corner of the room, calling out his name, but there was no response, only the echo of our own voices bouncing off the walls.

Alok's urgency was palpable as we rushed back down the stairs, searching every room of the house, hoping to find any trace of his father. But the house remained still, as if it held its secrets close, refusing to reveal the whereabouts of the man who had been its pillar for so long.

We enlisted the help of neighbours, friends, and even the local authorities. The same routine of reporting a missing person began anew, but this time it was a familiar ache that gnawed at our hearts. The uncertainty of not knowing where he was, whether he was safe, or if he was even alive, weighed heavily on us.

Alok and I searched tirelessly, combing through every inch of the house, scouring the nearby areas, and retracing the paths he might have taken. But it was as if he had evaporated into thin air, leaving behind only the lingering traces of his existence.

Days turned into a blur as we navigated the relentless passage of time without any signs of Alok's father. The routine of reporting to the police, answering their questions, and hoping for some form of closure became our new reality. Our home, once a sanctuary of familiarity, was now steeped in an unsettling uncertainty.

The police combed through every inch of the house, searching for clues that might hint at his whereabouts. Neighbours were questioned, and the local community buzzed with concern. The walls that had borne witness to decades of shared moments and familial love now echoed with the unanswered question of where he had gone.

In a desperate bid to reach beyond the confines of our immediate surroundings, we turned to the media, sharing his photographs and information in newspapers. The faces that once gazed at us with smiles from those photographs now stared back with a haunting absence, a reminder of the uncertainty that had woven its way into our lives.

Every phone call, every stranger's face, every knock at the door carried with it the hope that it might bring news of his whereabouts. But each day ended in a painful silence, the weight of his absence settling deeper within us. The community's concern shifted from sympathy to resignation, as the days stretched into weeks without a trace.

As the world outside continued with its rhythms, our lives seemed suspended in a state of perpetual uncertainty. The once-familiar corners of our home now held an emptiness that mirrored our hearts. Our memories, conversations, and shared experiences echoed with a poignant absence that refused to be ignored.

With each passing day, the mystery deepened, and the shadows of our concerns grew longer. Alok's father, once the bedrock of our lives, had vanished into thin air, leaving behind a void that was both tangible and intangible. And in the midst of this uncertainty, our search for answers continued, fuelled by the hope that someday, somehow, he would return and the pieces of this enigmatic puzzle would finally fall into place.

One Evening, at dinner table as Alok spoke those words, the weight of his emotions hung heavy in the air. The dining table that had witnessed countless meals, discussions, and moments of togetherness now held a conversation laden with the burden of unspoken truths. His decision to shift his parents' belongings and donate his father's possessions carried a mix of practicality and emotional turmoil that seemed to encapsulate his complex relationship with his father.

With every word he uttered, it became clear that Alok's struggle went beyond the physical act of rearranging belongings. He grappled with his identity as a son, navigating the shifting dynamics of dependence and independence that his father's absence had brought into sharp focus. His acknowledgement of other people's closure through the final rites underscored the profound absence he felt in his own life – an absence that defied easy categorization.

The legacy of comfort and privilege that Alok's father had provided was intertwined with an emotional distance that had persisted for years. The wealth amassed through meticulous financial planning and investments was juxtaposed against the intangible wealth of emotional bonds and connections that had eluded them. Alok's father had been the architect of their material stability, but the emotional foundations of their relationship had remained largely unexplored.

As Alok spoke of donating his father's belongings, it was as if he sought to cleanse the house of the lingering remnants of his father's presence – a presence that had often felt more like a shadow than a guiding light. His words resonated with the weight of years of unspoken expectations, unfulfilled hopes, and the heavy mantle of paternal responsibility that had been thrust upon him.

In that moment, the dining room seemed to contain the echoes of generations – the aspirations of a father who had built a life of comfort, the struggles of a son who had lived in its shelter, and the unspoken narratives that had been woven between them. As the dishes were cleared and the table sat empty, the room held the unspoken question of whether Alok's act of shifting and donating could truly clear the emotional clutter that lingered between them or if the complexities of their relationship would remain imprinted on the walls, forever seeking resolution.

Alok wanted a fresh start indeed

Alok: Asha, I've been thinking a lot about our house lately. With everything that has happened, I believe it's time for a change.

Asha: What do you mean, Alok?

Alok: Well, let's be honest, this place holds so many memories – both good and bad. But now that both of our parents are no longer with us, and we don't use the upper floor anymore, I feel like it's time to breathe new life into this house. What do you think about renovating the ground floor?

Asha: Renovating? That's a big step, Alok. But I understand what you're saying. It's like giving ourselves a fresh start, a new chapter in our lives.

Alok: Exactly. We've been through so much, Asha. From the unexpected disappearances to the losses we've faced, it's taken a toll on us. We're both in our 50s now, and we deserve to live a life that's full of happiness and positivity. We've faced enough trauma – it's time to bring some joy back into this house.

Asha: I agree, Alok. Our life has been quite a rollercoaster, and I believe renovating the house could be a way to symbolize moving forward. But it's a big decision, and it will require planning and effort.

Alok: I know, and I'm ready for that. We've saved up enough, and honestly, we don't have the burden of saving for children's education or anything like that. It's just the two of us now, and I want us to live comfortably and happily.

Asha: It's a fresh perspective, Alok. And it makes sense. Our house has been a witness to so much – our joys and sorrows. If renovating it can help us create new memories and find peace, then I'm on board.

The following months turned out to be unexpectedly busy for us. We were fully engaged in shifting the old belongings and furniture to the unused upper floor, making room for the upcoming renovation. One day, while sorting through Alok's father's wardrobe to gather old clothes for donation, I stumbled upon something astonishing – hidden amidst the clothes were envelopes, neatly tucked away. I called Alok over to take a look. Together, we opened the envelopes, and to our utter surprise, we discovered that they contained bundles of *cash. Alok started counting, and as the numbers added up, we realized that we were holding nearly 30 lakhs rupees in our hands.*

The year was 1980 when these notes were stashed away, and considering inflation and economic changes, this sum would be equivalent to around 1 crore rupees today. It was a shock, a revelation that we hadn't expected. We were left speechless, staring at the cash in disbelief. The very same wardrobe that had held his father's everyday clothes was now revealing a hidden treasure that had been tucked away for decades.

The discovery added a layer of complexity to our thoughts. The mystery surrounding Alok's father's actions deepened — why had he hidden such a significant amount of money? What was his intention?

As I held those bundles of cash in my hands, the pieces of the puzzle seemed to fall into place. Alok's mother's words echoed in my mind — the suspicion that Alok's father had acquired his wealth through unethical means, through bribes and other questionable methods. Could this hidden money be a testament to that? Could it be that Alok's father had secretly stashed away his ill-gotten gains, perhaps burdened by guilt or fear?

The idea was both unsettling and intriguing. It was as if the house itself was unveiling its secrets layer by layer, revealing a side of Alok's father that we had never known. The sudden revelation of this hidden wealth added another dimension to the complex tapestry of our lives at Shanti Villa. It was yet another unexpected turn, a new thread that we had to untangle amidst the mysteries that had surrounded us for so long.

Alok said , so Asha I think I don't need to use my savings then ,this amount is more than enough to use for renovation and furniture we wanted.

Alok's intention about the hidden stash of money left me momentarily speechless. The magnitude of the amount was staggering, and yet the context in which it was discovered added an eerie sense of unease to the situation. As I looked at Alok, who was processing the discovery himself, I found my voice.

"Alok," I began, my tone a mixture of concern and uncertainty, "this money, it's significant, no doubt. But do we really know where it came from? Your mother's fears, the suspicions she had — they all seem to converge here. What if this money is a testament to something we're not aware of? Could it be tied to the unsettling occurrences that have happened in this house?"

Alok's response came with a mixture of frustration and determination. He looked at me with a furrowed brow and a touch of incredulity, as if my words were pushing against his practical reasoning.

"Asha, what nonsense are you talking about?" he retorted, his tone slightly sharp. "Are you suggesting that we should burn this money or just leave it untouched? Come on, be realistic. We've discovered a significant amount here, and only a fool would reject such a fortune."

I could see that my concerns had collided head-on with Alok's enthusiasm to seize the opportunity. He continued, his voice firm, "I'm not going to let this opportunity slip away. I'm going to use this money for the renovation and furniture we've been wanting. And as for the remaining amount, I'll consult Mr.Ketan Pathak, our CA, and your neighbour and friend Chaya's husband. He is an expert, Dada used to consult him only for financial advice and I trust their advice. Please give me Chaya's house phone number so I can discuss this with them."

His words carried a determined conviction that left little room for debate. Alok's practical mindset clashed with my apprehensions, making it clear that we stood at a crossroads where decisions needed to be made. As he awaited Chaya's phone number, I found myself pondering the weight of our choices – whether to embrace the windfall with open arms or tread more carefully through the shadows of uncertainty that surrounded it. Finally I gave up.

The decision to renovate the ground floor of Shanti Villa marked a turning point in our lives. With Alok's determination and the newfound funds, we embarked on a journey to transform the space into something vibrant and filled with life. The process was a blend of excitement and nostalgia, as we bid farewell to the old and welcomed the new.

We began by clearing out the clutter and carefully packing away Alok's father's belongings that held years of memories. The empty space presented a blank canvas for our vision. Alok and I spent hours discussing layouts, designs, and color schemes, considering every detail to create a space that reflected our personalities and aspirations.

The renovation process started with structural changes. We knocked down walls to create an open-concept living area, allowing natural light to flood the space. Alok was hands-on, overseeing contractors and workers as they laid the foundation for our dreams. The sound of hammers, drills, and saws became the rhythm of transformation, signifying progress and change.

New flooring brought a fresh feel to the rooms, and the walls were painted in soothing, modern shades that resonated with both of us. The living room became a comfortable space with cozy seating, vibrant artwork, and bookshelves displaying our eclectic collection of books. Alok's father's antique furniture was shifted on the upper floor, seamlessly blending with our contemporary choices.

The kitchen underwent a complete makeover, with modern appliances, granite countertops, and ample storage. It became a place where I could unleash my culinary creativity while cherishing the legacy of those who had cooked in this very space before me.

The bedrooms were designed to be serene havens, each reflecting our individual tastes. The study area was equipped with the latest technology, a nod to Alok's interests and career. And the dining room became a place where we hosted gatherings, creating new memories around the table.

As the renovation neared its completion, the once-empty rooms now echoed with our laughter, conversations, and the promise of a new chapter. The transformation was more than just a physical change; it was a reflection of our journey, our dreams, and the love that bound us together. The old and the new intertwined seamlessly, capturing the essence of Shanti Villa's evolution.

Looking back, I couldn't help but ponder over the words Alok's mother had once spoken. Had I become complacent in the comfort of luxury and wealth? Was I, in my pursuit of a better life, unknowingly stepping on the ashes of others' dreams and hopes? The innocent girl who once entered Shanti Villa was now a woman who had embraced its opulence and grandeur.

At 19, I had embarked on a new phase of life, not fully aware of the complexities that lay ahead. The years flew by, and with them came success, happiness, but also loss and pain. The sudden twists of fate had transformed me from a sheltered daughter into the owner of a grand estate. But with this transformation came questions – questions about the sources of our wealth, the decisions made, and the consequences of our actions.

What if we hadn't used that money that we found hidden away in Alok's father's wardrobe? Could we have averted the bad karma that seemed to be trailing us? Could we have escaped the weight of guilt and the fear of unknown forces that Alok's mother had sensed? These questions haunted me as I stood at the crossroads of life, on the cusp of turning 50 that time.

Now when I am writing this diary, when I am about to turn 70 next year As I navigated the intricacies of aging, I found myself grappling with a deeper understanding of the choices we make and their far-reaching impacts. The wealth and luxury that I had embraced with open arms now felt like a burden, a reminder of the potential consequences of actions left unchecked. With age came wisdom, and with wisdom came the realization that material possessions could not replace the peace of mind that comes from living a life free from the shackles of guilt and regret.

As I looked around Shanti Villa, I wondered if the grandeur had overshadowed the essence of what truly mattered – love, kindness, and compassion. Perhaps there was still time to make amends, to ensure that the rest of my journey was guided by a moral compass that aimed for a balance between prosperity and integrity. The girl who once saw the world with innocent eyes was now a woman who had the power to choose her path wisely, to rewrite her story with a consciousness of the past and a commitment to a more meaningful future.

After the renovations were complete, Alok and I found ourselves stepping into a new chapter of our lives. With Alok's retirement on the horizon, we decided it was time to embrace a more active and social lifestyle. We joined a club near our house, which provided us with a platform to connect with like-minded individuals. Through this club, we formed new friendships that added vibrancy to our otherwise quiet existence.

With newfound companions, we began to indulge in monthly trips and outings. Exploring new places, experiencing new cultures, and creating memories together gave us a sense of rejuvenation and purpose. These adventures brought us closer as a couple, filling our lives with shared experiences and moments of joy.

Chhaya, our neighbor and friend, introduced me to a Kitty group – a gathering of ladies who met weekly to share stories, tea, and snacks. The camaraderie among us was heartwarming, and the regular meetups provided a welcome break from the solitude of our home. Through these gatherings, I not only found companionship but also a sense of belonging to a community of women who were navigating their own second innings in life.

Time flew by, and a decade passed as we immersed ourselves in this new lifestyle. Our once lonely lives were now filled with laughter, conversations, and meaningful interactions. The luxurious Shanti Villa, which once echoed with loneliness and secrets, was now a hub of social connections and cherished memories.

As we embraced the changes that life had thrown our way, I couldn't help but reflect on the journey I had undertaken. From a reluctant bride to a contented woman, I had evolved in ways I never imagined. The twists and turns, the losses and gains – they had all shaped me into a person who had learned to appreciate the value of relationships, the importance of living in the present, and the significance of using our blessings for the betterment of others.

With each passing day, I felt a renewed sense of purpose, knowing that our choices could influence not only our lives but the lives of those around us. As we enjoyed our second innings together, I couldn't help but be grateful for the unexpected turns that had led us here, to a life filled with companionship, laughter, and the warmth of newfound friendships.

As time passed by A noticeable shift began to take place in our lives, catching me off guard. Alok, who was once a social and outgoing individual, gradually started to distance himself from the vibrant social activities that had become an integral part of our routine. It was as if a curtain had been drawn between him and the world outside.

The gatherings, the trips, the camaraderie that had brought us so much joy, suddenly seemed to lose their appeal for Alok. He started to spend more and more time in his study, engrossed in books and research. His withdrawal was palpable, and I couldn't help but wonder about the reason behind this sudden change. As his partner, I was torn between giving him space and reaching out to understand his perspective. I respected his need for solitude but also felt concerned about the emotional distance that seemed to be growing between us. Our life, which had been filled with shared moments and laughter, was now experiencing a shift that left me feeling uncertain.

I longed to bridge the gap and reconnect with the Alok I had known – the one who was open, engaging, and full of life. Yet, I also recognized the importance of allowing him the time and space he needed to navigate this new phase.

The sight of the newly acquired books on Alok's study shelves sent a ripple of surprise and curiosity through me. The collection seemed to be a blend of two contrasting worlds – one focusing on the intricate workings of the human mind and the other delving into the mystical realms of witchcraft and tantra vidya. It was a juxtaposition that puzzled and intrigued me.

I found myself wondering about the motivations behind this eclectic selection. What had prompted Alok to dive into the depths of psychology and the subconscious mind, seeking to unravel the intricacies of human behavior and thought processes? And what had drawn him towards the mystique of witchcraft and tantra vidya, subjects that often carried an air of enigma and the unknown?

As I observed him engrossed in his reading, I couldn't help but reflect on the transformations our lives had undergone over the years. From the moment we stepped into Shanti Villa to the mysteries that had unfolded within its walls, our journey had been marked by unexpected turns and revelations. And now, as Alok ventured into the uncharted territories of the mind and metaphysical realms.

The psychology volumes provided a glimpse into the complexities of human thought patterns, shedding light on the inner workings of the mind. The witchcraft and tantra vidya texts, on the other hand, offered a glimpse into practices that held a mystic allure, filled with rituals, symbols, and ancient wisdom.

As days turned into weeks, I watched Alok immerse himself in his studies with an intensity I had rarely seen before. He seemed driven by a quest for knowledge, a hunger to understand the depths of both the conscious and subconscious mind. His conversations, once reserved and distant, now revolved around his discoveries and insights from his readings.

Despite my initial reservations, I realized that this phase was his way of seeking answers, exploring the uncharted territories of the mind and spirit. And while I may not have fully comprehended the reasons behind his choices, I respected his need for this journey of self-discovery.

In the midst of the daily routines that had become our lives, a shift occurred that sent ripples of concern through my heart. Alok's behavior had transformed into something I had never anticipated – he began to withdraw further into himself. His study, once a place of shared discussions and intellectual pursuits, now became his sanctuary. The lines between day and night blurred for him, as he started sleeping and eating amidst the stacks of books and research materials that had overtaken the room.

Then came a day that intensified my worries. A group of individuals, dressed in an air of mystery and led by a person cloaked in black, arrived at our doorstep. Their arrival felt as though a cloud of unease had settled over Shanti Villa. The leader held a large mala in his hands, a symbol of spirituality? that held an air of gravity. Three others accompanied him, seemingly assistants or companions.

As they were ushered in, Alok took them directly to the upper floor – a part of our house that had remained untouched and unused since his father's disappearance. This gesture signalled a shift in his focus, as if he had found solace in this untouched space. Their purpose and their connection to Alok remained shrouded in mystery, and I found myself grappling with both curiosity and concern.

In the past, our home had been a place of shared experiences, a sanctuary where both of us had come together to navigate the challenges life had presented us. But now, it felt as though a divide had emerged, a barrier that kept us from understanding each other's journeys.

As I stood on the periphery of this unfolding scenario, a sense of isolation deepened within me. Alok's transformation and the presence of these enigmatic visitors had left me feeling like an outsider in my own home. And as days turned into nights, I found myself grappling with questions that seemed to have no easy answers – questions about Alok's path, the purpose of these visitors, and the future that lay ahead for both of us.

The arrival of the visitors sent an unsettling ripple through the atmosphere of our home. Their demeanour, draped in an air of mystery and apprehension, stood in stark contrast to the usual flow of our lives. Among them was a figure adorned in black garments, bearing a substantial mala in their hands, the others seemingly accompanying them as assistants. Their purpose and intent were shrouded in uncertainty, and their sudden appearance raised questions that scratched at the edges of my thoughts.

Alok's reaction to their arrival only deepened my concerns. Without a word, he led them up the staircase to the upper floor, a gesture that felt distant and foreign. As the door closed behind them, a sense of isolation settled around me. The house, once a haven of shared moments and companionship, now felt estranged, the walls echoing with an emptiness that resonated with my unease.

I paced through the living spaces, my footsteps accompanied by the disquieting silence that had enveloped the house. The questions accumulated like shadows in my mind – who were these visitors, and what connection did they hold to Alok's newfound interests? His retreat to the upper floor with them stirred a mix of confusion and concern, leaving me on the periphery of an unfolding situation I struggled to comprehend.

Hours seemed to stretch into infinity as I waited, my restlessness growing with every passing minute. Eventually, the door opened, and Alok emerged, his face bearing traces of an encounter that had left its mark. His eyes held a distant intensity, and his demeanour seemed transformed, as though he had ventured beyond the realms of our shared reality.

Attempts to engage him in conversation proved futile. His responses were short, his words veiled in layers of secrecy that pushed me further away. The chasm that had grown between us during this phase had now expanded into an abyss, a divide I struggled to bridge as I grappled with my concerns and fears.

As the day waned into evening, Alok retreated once again to his study, leaving me alone with the weight of unanswered questions. The visitors' cryptic presence and the secrets that had passed between them gnawed at my thoughts, leaving me entangled in a web of uncertainty.

In the midst of this unfolding enigma, I found myself longing for the connection we had once shared, the bond that had weathered life's trials and tribulations. But as darkness settled over Shanti Villa, I was left with the sobering realization that our paths had diverged, and the answers I sought seemed to elude me, hidden within the shadows of Alok's reticence.

"And the darkest day of my life arrived - it was 13th June 2010. Alok disappeared from our residence."

As the morning sunlight filtered through the curtains, I stirred from my sleep and embarked on my usual routine. It had become a habit, an unspoken understanding, that Alok must have spent the night engrossed in his study. Laxmi, our reliable house help, arrived promptly and began attending to her tasks. As she bustled about the house, I made my way to the study, my steps guided by a sense of familiarity. But today, that familiarity was disrupted. A sense of unease began to creep in as I scanned the room — the desk littered with books; the chair pushed back slightly — but Alok was nowhere to be found. My growing concern led me to check the washroom, the dining area, and every corner of the house, yet his absence persisted, shrouding the morning in an unsettling feeling.

With a mix of trepidation and determination, I grabbed a courage to explore the upper floor, to check Alok's presence, the very place that had been the epicenter of Alok's secretive interactions with those unsettling individuals. Laxmi, my constant companion, accompanied me as we climbed the stairs, every step heavy with the memories of Ma's disappearance. That was the time when I had last visited this place. My heart raced, and I pushed back the negative thoughts, urging myself to continue. The upper floor was draped in a cloak of dust and silence, a stark contrast to its previous life. My mind drifted to Ma's warnings, her unease about this house, and a shiver ran down my spine.

Summoning my courage, I began to search each room, a flood of memories from years past surging through my mind. The eeriness of the moment was undeniable, but I persisted. As I approached the nursery, in my memory we had locked the door permanently but here the door stood wide open. My heart raced as I entered, my eyes taking in the scene before me.

As we moved through the rooms, I noticed something unusual – the nursery, once locked and abandoned, stood open. My heart raced as I stepped inside, my eyes widening at the unexpected sight before me. The room, once empty, now held a wooden mahogany table and three chairs, arranged as if for a meeting. The tableau was incongruous with my memory of the room, and a chill ran down my spine. The air seemed charged with a strange energy, and a sense of foreboding settled over me.

finally converging in this eerie moment. What had happened in this room? What had Alok been involved in? And where was he now? The room stood as a silent witness, offering no answers, only an unsettling sense of mystery that seemed to thicken the air around me.

Lost in my thoughts and the peculiar sight of the rearranged room, I barely noticed Laxmi's gentle nudge. Her suggestion to check the attic, a place I had always avoided, brought a mixture of apprehension and curiosity. However, my hesitation was evident, and Laxmi, being the resolute person she was, decided to investigate on her own.

As she returned with a crestfallen expression, the truth seemed to crystallize before me – Alok had disappeared, just like Ma and Dada. The mystery that had woven itself around our lives had now consumed my husband as well. The weight of it all settled heavily on my shoulders, and a sense of helplessness engulfed me.

Deep down, I recognized the truth I was reluctant to face – Alok was gone, and this time, he had joined the enigmatic vanishing act that had plagued Shanti Villa for so long. My heart ached with a mixture of sorrow, confusion, and frustration. The house that had once been a source of comfort and stability had transformed into a place of mystery and tragedy.

The rising panic gripped me as I realized the uncanny resemblance between this situation and the past disappearances – first Ma, then Dada, and now Alok. The feeling of isolation weighed heavily on me, making me long for the presence of my loved ones ++who were now inexplicably absent. Amid the turmoil of my thoughts, Laxmi reached out for help, contacting Chhaya, a neighbor and a dear friend. Chhaya arrived accompanied by her husband, Mr. Ketan, who was not only Alok's CA but also a trusted confidant. Their reassuring presence brought a semblance of comfort, as Chhaya gently urged me to collect my thoughts. The era had advanced enough for us to own mobile phones, but I had never embraced the technology. Alok had a cellphone, but it was locked away in his study – a barrier between me and potential answers. Chhaya and Ketan's support were a lifeline in this storm of uncertainty, offering me stability in a time of upheaval.

As we gathered in the dining room, Chhaya's concern was palpable. She instructed Laxmi to prepare coffee for me, a gesture went unnoticed by my numb mind. As the aroma of the brewing coffee filled the air, my mind was a whirlwind of emotions. The absence of Alok felt like an immense void, and the reality of facing life without him at this stage of our lives was overwhelming.

In moments like these, when death strikes through unexpected circumstances, there's no closure, no understanding to grasp. I realized that history had repeated itself within the walls of Shanti Villa for the third time. The disappearances of Ma, Dada, and now Alok seemed to be a tragic pattern that defied explanation. Questions swirled in my mind, but answers remained elusive.

Amidst the heaviness in the room, Ketan's voice broke the silence. He expressed a desire to conduct one final search of the house before involving the police, hoping to uncover any clue or message Alok might have left behind. I nodded, my heart heavy with the realization that there was little else I could do but wait for whatever news would come.

Chhaya's words resonated with a sense of care and concern that brought a glimmer of comfort to the chaos of my thoughts. She gently inquired if I had eaten or taken my blood pressure medication, reminding me of the need to take care of myself during these trying times. Her compassionate advice struck a chord, making me realize that I was indeed allowing my fears and the history of the house to cloud my judgment and emotions.

Her encouragement to remain positive and open to the possibility that Alok might return brought a brief moment of hope amidst the uncertainty. It was a reminder that, no matter the circumstances, I had to maintain my own well-being in order to face whatever was to come.

After half an hour, Ketan reappeared in the dining room, holding a file that appeared to be from a hospital, containing medical records and test reports. His words were laden with a mix of curiosity and concern as he addressed me directly. "Asha, I found these medical records hidden under the couch in Alok's study. It seems like he was undergoing treatment for the past three years. Do you have any idea what happened to Alok?"

His revelation hit me like a sudden jolt, and I was left speechless for a moment. My mind raced to comprehend the implications of what Ketan had just shared. Alok had been seeking medical treatment without my knowledge, keeping his health struggles a secret. The feeling of shock was quickly replaced by a mixture of emotions – surprise, hurt, and a hint of betrayal. How had our connection deteriorated to a point where he felt compelled to hide such a significant aspect of his life from me?

As I met Ketan's gaze, my voice quivered slightly, "I had no idea he was going through this. How could he keep something so important hidden from me for so long?" The realization that Alok had carried this burden alone, without reaching out for my support, weighed heavily on my heart. It was a stark reminder that we had grown distant, and the intimacy that had once defined our relationship had eroded over time.

"What does it say? What kind of health issue was he suffering from?" I inquired, my voice tinged with concern and anxiety. I needed to understand what Alok had been facing all this time, a reality he had chosen to keep hidden.

Ketan looked at me with a somber expression, his voice carrying the weight of the revelation he was about to share. "Asha, it's not a physical issue that he was dealing with," he said, his tone heavy. "He was consulting a psychologist, Dr. Manish Rathi."

His words hit me like a shockwave, leaving me stunned and struggling to process their significance. The revelation that Alok had been seeking help for mental and emotional challenges was unexpected and alarming. I felt a mix of emotions – empathy for what he must have been going through, regret for not having been there to support him, and a growing sense of urgency to understand the depth of his struggles.

My mind raced as I tried to grasp the reality of the situation. Why did he keep it hidden? Was he ashamed or afraid of sharing his emotional turmoil with me? And more importantly, how had I failed to notice the signs that he was grappling with something so profound? As my thoughts swirled, a new layer of complexity was added to the enigma of our lives in Shanti Villa.

Ketan's actions mirrored my growing concern. He also retrieved Alok's cellphone from the study and dialed the numbers stored in his contacts, hoping against hope that someone might have information about Alok's whereabouts. But it lead to the obvious disappointment each conversation led to a dead end, the realization sank in that Alok had truly disappeared without a trace.

The weight of the situation pressed down on us, and the absence of any leads deepened the mystery. Alok's sudden withdrawal, his clandestine visits from those enigmatic individuals, and now this revelation of his emotional struggles painted a picture I could scarcely comprehend.

In the dimly lit solitude of the night, the weight of my reality bore down on me. With Chaya and Ketan's unwavering support, we had taken the step to register a formal complaint about Alok's unexplained disappearance. I was now all too familiar with the process, the questions, the official statements—steps that had been taken not long ago for Alok's parents. It was an eerie sense of déjà vu, a twisted echo of the past that had turned into a nightmarish present.

Chaya remained by my side like a guardian angel, offering her strength and companionship. But as the day surrendered to night and Chaya left, the silence around me grew louder, magnifying the emptiness that enveloped Shanti Villa. The truth was undeniable: Alok's absence had cast me into a void, one where the vast expanse of our once-lively home only emphasized my solitude.

The tears came, relentless and unstoppable. In the midst of my sorrow, I found myself yearning for the presence of Alok, whose distance had grown even before his mysterious disappearance. I cried not only for his absence, but for the distance that had crept between us, the secrets that had hidden his inner turmoil, and the uncertainty that now consumed my every thought.

As the night stretched on, the tears flowed freely, each drop carrying with it the weight of our shared history, our joys and sorrows, and the unspoken bond that had been tested beyond measure. Shanti Villa, once a symbol of comfort and togetherness, now echoed with the sound of my solitude, a stark reminder of the journey I was navigating through the uncharted territories of grief and uncertainty.

My thoughts whirled, grappling with the uncertainty and the burden of not knowing what was happening in Alok's life. How long had he been seeing a psychologist? What had driven him to such lengths of secrecy? And most importantly, where could he be now?

As the hours ticked by, every moment felt like an eternity, each second dripping with unanswered questions and escalating anxiety. The enigma of Shanti Villa had taken a sinister turn, leaving me desperate for answers and haunted by the thought of what could have befallen Alok in the midst of his struggles.

The morning light seeped through the curtains, casting a faint glow on the walls of the bedroom. Yet, the light that had once filled my days felt dimmed, overshadowed by the weight of Alok's unexplained absence. I lay still for a moment, dreading the emptiness that awaited me beyond the confines of my bed.

With a deep sigh, I reluctantly pushed myself up, my limbs heavy with both exhaustion and the weight of my thoughts. As I swung my legs over the edge of the bed, the reality of the situation struck me anew—Alok was not here. There would be no shared laughter over breakfast, no discussions about plans for the day, no morning tea enjoyed together.

The thought was suffocating, yet the ringing of the doorbell pulled me from my reverie. I rose, albeit with reluctance, and made my way to the door. Laxmi, our faithful house help, stood there with her usual warm smile, a beacon of familiarity in a world that suddenly felt alien. Her presence was a reminder that life continued to move forward, even in the face of heartache and uncertainty.

As I went about the motions of the morning—preparing breakfast, making tea—I couldn't help but feel the hollowness of my actions. The routine that had once been so familiar now felt disjointed, as if a crucial piece was missing. The aroma of the food, the clinking of utensils, and the sound of the boiling kettle were all echoes of a life that had been abruptly altered.

While my body went through the motions, my mind wandered through the memories of the countless mornings Alok and I had spent together. The shared jokes, the gentle teasing, the comfortable silence—it all seemed like a distant dream now. And as I set the table, a painful realization hit me: Alok's absence wasn't just about the physical space he left behind, but the void he had created in the very fabric of our shared existence.

As I sat down to eat breakfast, the food tasted bland, the flavors muted by the heaviness in my heart. The once-familiar sounds of cutlery against plates were accompanied by a deafening silence that seemed to echo Alok's absence. Yet, in the midst of this emptiness, I knew I had to keep moving forward. The morning had dawned, and life was demanding that I face it, even in the absence of the one person who had been an integral part of it.

The bell rang again this time Ketan and Chaya had arrived to check on me, i asked Lakshmi to serve them breakfast and tea. As we sat together, the words exchanged were few, but the unspoken bond of camaraderie spoke volumes. Chaya and Ketan's presence were a lifeline, a reminder that even in the midst of the darkest moments, human connection and compassion could provide a glimmer of hope.

Ketan's voice brought me back to the present, reminding me of the task at hand. He informed me that the police inspector would be coming by to conduct a routine check of Alok's belongings. Nodding in acknowledgment, I prepared myself mentally for their visit.

It wasn't long before two police officers arrived at our doorstep. The inspector introduced himself and his colleague before beginning the inquiry. His questions were methodical, seeking to understand the context of Alok's disappearance and gather any potential leads.

Seated in the living room, the inspector's gaze was probing yet empathetic. He wanted to know if we had any reason to believe that Alok had been threatened or if there were any enemies he might have had. I answered each question truthfully, recounting the details of Alok's recent behavior and any unusual occurrences in the house.

As the questions continued, I couldn't shake the feeling that this investigation was eerily similar to the ones that had taken place during Ma and Dada's disappearances. The repetition of the pattern only intensified the unsettling nature of the situation. It was a reminder of the past events that had shaped the history of Shanti Villa, events that seemed to defy explanation.

With every question answered, it became clearer that there were no apparent leads or clues to Alok's whereabouts. The inspector jotted down notes in his notebook, his expression a mix of professionalism and genuine concern. As the inquiry concluded, he assured me that they would do their best to find Alok and that we should stay in touch with them for any updates.

As the police officers left, a sense of unease settled over me once more. The familiarity of the investigation process was haunting, and the lack of answers only heightened my anxiety. I watched their retreating figures through the window, feeling a mixture of frustration and helplessness. My hope for closure and answers felt distant, and I was left to grapple with the uncertainty that had become an unwelcome companion in my life.

As the days turned into weeks since Alok's disappearance, Chaya's visits became a consistent source of support and companionship. Ketan, too, would drop by regularly to check on me, their presence alleviating the solitude that had settled in my home. One sunny day, as we sat in the garden sipping on our coffee, Ketan broached a topic that had been lingering in my thoughts.

"Asha," he began, his voice gentle, "it's been nearly a month now, and you've been alone in this big house. Have you considered the idea of renting out the upper floor? It could be a way to have some company and support, not just for the money."

His words struck a chord with me. I had been contemplating the same thought, especially in the wake of Alok's absence. While he was here, he valued his privacy, but now that he was gone, the house felt larger and quieter than ever. Ketan's suggestion seemed like a practical way to address both my need for companionship and the underutilized space.

I nodded thoughtfully, acknowledging that his suggestion had merit. "You might be right, Ketan. It's just that I'm not sure how to find a suitable family or tenants. And what if things don't work out?"

Ketan smiled reassuringly. "Don't worry, Asha. We can place an advertisement in the newspaper. People who are interested in renting a place will get in touch with you. You can meet them, see if it's a good fit, and if everything aligns, you can draft a rental agreement and I will help you through the process."

His words brought a sense of relief. Having Ketan's expertise and Chaya's support made the prospect of renting out the upper floor more manageable. It was a way to both address my newfound solitude and ensure that the space was utilized in a meaningful way. With their support, the idea transformed from a passing thought into a practical plan.

As our conversation continued, Chaya brought up another topic

Asha," she interjected gently, "I wanted to ask if you'd like to join us for a Satsang sandhya tomorrow. We believe that having spiritual support can provide solace and strength during difficult times. Tomorrow at 6 PM, a renowned Sadh guru named Govind Ji, who is a devoted follower of Lord Krishna, will be coming to lead the session."

Her invitation touched me. While I hadn't been particularly religious in the past, the recent events had made me reflect on the importance of finding solace and meaning in spiritual practices. The idea of attending a Satsang, a gathering focused on spiritual discourse and meditation, felt like a step in the right direction. It could offer me a sense of community and guidance during this challenging phase of my life.

"I appreciate the invitation, Chaya," I responded with sincerity. "Attending the Satsang sounds like a meaningful way to spend my time. I'll be glad to join you."

Chaya's warm smile reflected her genuine support, and I felt a renewed sense of connection with her and the spiritual path that she and Ketan had embraced. As I contemplated the upcoming Satsang, I realized that amidst the changes and uncertainties in my life, finding spiritual grounding and companionship could be a source of strength and comfort that I had been seeking.

The following evening, Chaya and Ketan arrived at my home to pick me up for the Satsang sandhya. As I stepped into their car, a sense of anticipation mixed with curiosity filled the air. We embarked on a journey that led us to a place that defied my expectations. The place was referred to as an Ashram, but it was unlike any traditional religious setting I had encountered before.

Upon arrival, I was pleasantly surprised to find that the Ashram seamlessly integrated modern amenities with a spiritual ambiance. The surroundings were serene and peaceful, adorned with lush trees and the soothing sounds of nature. The Ashram itself had various facilities – a laboratory where students engaged in scientific exploration, an open school nestled amidst the beauty of nature, a serene mandir, and a library that beckoned for intellectual exploration. This place was a harmonious fusion of science and spirituality, a testament to the evolving nature of our understanding of the world.

As we stepped inside, I felt a sense of serenity wash over me. The atmosphere was welcoming, and the people I saw were a diverse group – from young students engrossed in their studies to individuals of all ages who had come seeking spiritual nourishment. This Ashram seemed to offer a holistic approach to growth and development, acknowledging the significance of both material and spiritual aspects of life.

Chaya, Ketan, and I settled in for the Satsang sandhya, surrounded by an aura of openness, learning, and contemplation. The presence of this tranquil oasis in the midst of our bustling world gave me a renewed perspective on the potential for inner transformation and personal growth. As I listened to the discourse and participated in the meditative practices, I began to feel a sense of calm and unity, a reminder that amidst life's challenges, there are spaces that nurture the soul and offer solace.

Indeed, the Satsang sandhya at the Ashram was a gathering of diverse souls, transcending social and economic boundaries. As I looked around, I noticed people from various walks of life coming together under the same roof. It was a reflection of the universal human yearning for inner peace and spiritual fulfilment.

The attendees spanned generations – young children, eager to absorb wisdom beyond their years; middle-aged individuals seeking a refuge from the daily grind; and older participants, perhaps embarking on a journey of introspection in the twilight of their lives. The diversity in the crowd reminded me that the pursuit of inner peace is not confined to any particular stage of life or social status.

It was an eye-opening experience to witness how people from all backgrounds, be it the wealthy or the less privileged, had a shared aspiration for tranquillity and solace. The Ashram provided a sanctuary where these seekers could come together, leaving behind the external trappings that society often values. In this sacred space, the distinctions of wealth, power, and luxury seemed to fade into insignificance.

Sadhguru Govind Ji's appearance defied the traditional image I had held of spiritual leaders. He was unlike any guru I had encountered before – his demeanor exuded a youthful vibrancy and a modern outlook that contradicted the stereotypical attire and age-old appearances often associated with spiritual figures in our society.

Dressed in a crisp ironed cotton shirt and gray pants, Govind Ji carried an air of simplicity and authenticity. His spectacles perched on his eyes seemed to magnify not just his vision, but his insight into the complexities of life as well. His face radiated an unmistakable glow, reflecting a sense of inner peace and wisdom that surpassed his relatively young age. As he took his seat in the amphitheater, I couldn't help but feel intrigued by the stark contrast between his appearance and the preconceived notions I had harbored.

Chaya, who had sensed my surprise, offered an explanation with a knowing smile. She shared that Govind Ji was indeed an embodiment of the modern blend of spirituality and intellect. He held a degree in engineering, a background that he chose to set aside in pursuit of a deeper understanding of life's essence through the lens of our ancient vedas and shastras. In this choice, he found profound meaning and purpose, resonating with the timeless wisdom encoded within our scriptures.

As I sat there, watching Govind Ji engage with the audience, it became clear that his wisdom was rooted in a comprehensive understanding of both the material and spiritual dimensions of life. His talks reflected a profound grasp of our scriptures, philosophy, and science, which he seamlessly integrated to address the modern challenges faced by individuals today.

Listening to him speak, I realized that the image of a guru was evolving to encompass a wider spectrum of personalities and backgrounds. Govind Ji's presence broke down the barriers of traditional expectations, emphasizing that spiritual insight and guidance can come from individuals of all walks of life, transcending age, appearance, and societal norms.

During the satsang, Sadhguru Govind Ji delved into a profound discussion on a specific Adhyaya (chapter) from the Bhagavad Gita – Chapter 16. This chapter offers deep insights into the nature of human tendencies and their consequences, shedding light on the interplay between positive and negative qualities that shape our lives.

Govind Ji began by explaining the context of this chapter in the Bhagavad Gita. He emphasized that Lord Krishna's teachings are timeless and relevant to all ages, guiding individuals through the intricacies of life and providing a roadmap for spiritual growth and self-realization.

In Chapter 16 of the Gita, Lord Krishna delineates the characteristics of individuals driven by "asuric" or demonic tendencies. These traits are rooted in ignorance and ego, leading individuals down a path of darkness, suffering, and negative karma. Govind Ji highlighted the destructive nature of these tendencies, which include arrogance, anger, cruelty, deceit, and an insatiable desire for power. He eloquently described how these qualities not only harm others but also imprison those who possess them in a cycle of negativity and suffering.

Lord Krishna's teachings in this chapter underscore the profound link between our actions, intentions, and their consequences. Govind Ji emphasized that individuals who succumb to these negative traits become trapped in a web of bad karma, which not only affects their current life but also shapes their future lives. This understanding sheds light on the interconnected nature of existence and the accountability that each of us carries for our actions.

As Govind Ji elaborated on these teachings, I found myself drawn into a deeper contemplation of the intricate dynamics of human behavior and its impact. His insights illuminated the timeless wisdom contained within the Bhagavad Gita, offering a holistic perspective on the nature of good and evil, light and darkness.

The teachings of Chapter 16 served as a poignant reminder of the significance of self-awareness and conscious choices in our journey through life. Govind Ji guided us towards a path of introspection, encouraging us to assess our own tendencies and seek liberation from the shackles of negative traits. By recognizing the detrimental effects of these qualities and making a dedicated effort to overcome them, individuals can break free from the cycle of bad karma and progress towards spiritual growth and ultimate liberation.

Listening to Govind Ji's exposition, I felt a profound sense of awe and gratitude for the wisdom encapsulated within the Bhagavad Gita. The teachings of this chapter offered a transformative perspective on the intricacies of human nature and the choices that shape our destiny..

I was thinking Directly or indirectly ,whatever happened with us in Shanti Villa is Indeed a result of our bad karma,Though I was not directly linked with it but I have enjoyed the luxury and benefits arrived from those deeds.

As the satsang concluded, the atmosphere transitioned into an interactive session where attendees had the opportunity to seek guidance from Sadhguru Govind Ji regarding their personal challenges. It was fascinating to witness the diverse range of issues that people brought forth, seeking solutions rooted in spiritual wisdom.

One individual stood up and shared his predicament of facing losses in his business due to a cheating partner. Govind Ji's response was simple yet profound, reflecting his practical approach to spirituality. He recommended a solution that resonated with the principles of Vastu Shastra, a traditional Indian architectural science that emphasizes harmony between living spaces and their energy flow.

Govind Ji's solution was surprisingly uncomplicated – he suggested a change in the orientation of the individual's cabin. He advised the person to reposition the cabin to face the north-east direction, which is considered auspicious in Vastu Shastra. This orientation is believed to promote positive energies and enhance the overall well-being of individuals working in that space.

Additionally, Govind Ji recommended placing a jaggery box within the cabin. The symbolism behind this suggestion lies in the notion of offering sweetness to counterbalance the bitterness of the situation. Jaggery, a natural sweetener, is believed to symbolize positive intentions and the willingness to foster goodwill.

What struck me the most about Govind Ji's response was its simplicity and authenticity. Unlike some so-called spiritual solutions that involve elaborate rituals and hefty fees, Govind Ji's guidance was practical, accessible, and cost-effective. There was a genuine sense of integrity in his advice, devoid of any ulterior motives.

Observing the individual's grateful expression as he received this guidance, I realized that spiritual teachings don't need to be shrouded in complexity. True wisdom often lies in the simplicity of its application. Govind Ji's approach exemplified this concept, demonstrating that even the most intricate challenges can be addressed through small yet meaningful changes that align with the natural flow of energies.

Feeling inspired by the wisdom and guidance shared by Sadh guru Govind Ji, a thought started to take root in my mind. I began contemplating the idea of seeking his guidance for my own life's challenges. Recalling how my father's presence had brought a positive change to Shanti villa, dispelling negative energies and infusing the surroundings with a renewed sense of positivity, I wondered if Sadh guru Govind Ji could offer insights that might help me navigate my own journey.

With a mix of curiosity and hope, I considered reaching out to Sadhguru Govind Ji to discuss the challenges that had unfolded in Shanti villa over the years. The sudden disappearances and the repeated incidents of unsettling energies in the house left me seeking answers, seeking a path towards restoration and healing. As the satsang concluded and people began to disperse, I approached Chaya and asked her to accompany me. Govind Ji was in the process of leaving, yet he remained seated. His gaze seemed to linger on me, and an unspoken connection seemed to form between us. With

Chaya by my side, we approached and sat down in front of the Asana where Govind Ji was seated. There was a sense of anticipation in the air, as if he had been waiting for this moment.

As Govind Ji looked at me, his eyes held a depth of understanding and compassion. His presence felt calming and reassuring, as though he could see beyond the surface and into the heart of my concerns. With a gentle smile, he acknowledged my presence and broke the silence with words that held immense weight.

"I believe you have questions to ask?" Govind Ji's words were both direct and empathetic. It was as if he had already sensed the weight of my troubles and was offering a safe space for me to share my concerns. His tone held a warmth that invited honesty and vulnerability.

I returned his smile and nodded, grateful for the opportunity to finally voice my worries. With a mixture of apprehension and trust, I began to speak, "Govind Ji, my husband has been missing from our home for the past month. There are no signs of him leaving, and similarly, my in-laws have also disappeared. I don't know where to turn or what steps to take."

As I shared my situation, I felt a sense of release. It was as if the weight of my worries was gradually being lifted, and the act of sharing my concerns with Govind Ji felt like a balm for my troubled heart. His presence exuded an aura of tranquility, making it easier for me to open up about the uncertainties that had clouded my life.

With every word that I spoke, Govind Ji listened intently, his gaze unwavering and his demeanor radiating compassion. It was a conversation that transcended the boundaries of the ordinary, as if our souls were engaged in a dialogue that delved into the depths of existence itself. And as I concluded my story, I looked at Govind Ji, seeking guidance, solace, and perhaps even a glimmer of hope amidst the uncertainty that had enveloped my life.

Asha Ji, Govind Ji's voice resonated with an air of gravity as he began to speak, his words carrying an unusual weight. His eyes seemed to hold a depth of knowledge that extended far beyond the realm of ordinary understanding. With a sense of intrigue mixed with trepidation, I leaned in to listen closely.

"In the vast tapestry of the universe, there exists a dimension parallel to the one we inhabit," Govind Ji's voice grew even more solemn. "In this parallel dimension, the very same entities exist—people, objects, and places—but they manifest in a different manner, often taking on a sinister form. This dimension is not bound by the same laws that govern our world, and it harbors an unsettling presence."

The room seemed to grow still as Govind Ji's words hung in the air, and an unsettling feeling began to take root within me. His explanation seemed to blur the lines between reality and the inexplicable, plunging me into a realm of uncertainty that I had never fathomed before.

"The occurrences that have transpired in your life are undeniably tragic," Govind Ji continued, his expression unwavering. "However, providing answers to your questions is not a task that can be accomplished easily. Moreover, the revelations you seek may not be as comforting as you anticipate."and at this age I don't know if you will be able to handle it He said.

Furthermore, Govind Ji's words carried a sense of responsibility and empowerment. "I can offer you guidance, Asha Ji," he continued, his gaze steady and unwavering, "but ultimately, the journey is yours to undertake. Just as Lord Krishna guided Arjuna on the battlefield, I can be your guide, illuminating the path before you. Yet, the choices you make and the steps you take are yours alone."

His comparison to the profound conversation between Lord Krishna and Arjuna resonated deeply within me. The notion of Govind Ji being a guide, a Sarathi, mirrored the divine guidance that Lord Krishna had provided to Arjuna during the Mahabharata..

Govind Ji's advice resonated deeply with me. His words carried a profound sense of guidance, an anchor amidst the tumultuous uncertainty that surrounded me. "Asha Ji," he began, his tone gentle yet firm, "before embarking on any battle, one must first assess the opponent. Similarly, before you face the enigma that has gripped your life, take a step back and understand the nature of what you are up against."

I listened intently, my curiosity piqued. "What do I need to do?" I inquired, eager to know the path he was suggesting. His reply was both simple and intriguing. "Consider the role of spirituality in your life," he said, "How often do you engage in daily rituals, in worship?" I explained that while Ma and Dada used to conduct regular rituals, and Alok did as well until recent times, I had become disconnected from these practices. My faith had wavered, and my connection to spirituality had weakened.

In response, Govind Ji gently offered his guidance. "Asha Ji, I urge you to make a change. Incorporate a daily pooja into your routine. Spirituality can be your greatest shield and ally in times of challenge. Light a Diya and incense stick, offer Bhog and flowers to the divine every morning and evening. This simple act of devotion can help you reconnect with the spiritual realm and restore your faith."

But there was more to his plan. With a contemplative pause, he continued, "And when you feel ready, take an additional step. Light a diya from the existing one in your mandir, one that is already illuminated with the power of your devotion. Take a portion of the Bhog you offer and you also eat it. Place these items in your upper floor, perhaps near its entrance or within its confines. Allow the energies of your devotion to linger there."

His guidance struck a chord within me. It was both practical and symbolic, a way to bridge the gap between the unknown and the familiar. As he spoke, a sense of purpose and determination stirred within me. Heeding Govind Ji's words, I envisioned myself carrying out these rituals, offering my prayers with sincerity, and imbuing my surroundings with the light of devotion.

His final words were laden with anticipation, "In time, Asha Ji, you will find your answers. Just as light dispels darkness, the power of your faith can unveil the truths you seek." In that moment, I embraced his advice, recognizing it as a path towards unraveling the mysteries that had plagued my existence.

In his words, I sensed a warning with —that by embracing this ritual, I might uncover truths that had eluded me for far too long. It was an unconventional approach, one that mingled spirituality with intuition, invoking the ancient wisdom of rituals to address contemporary challenges.

As the tranquil atmosphere of the Satsang lingered in my thoughts, I returned home, engrossed in a mix of emotions. The air seemed infused with a renewed energy, a sense of purpose that echoed Govind Ji's words. Upon stepping through the door, the ringing of the landline broke the silence. I answered, intrigued by the unexpected call.

The voice on the other end introduced herself as Pallavi Deshmukh. She had come across the advertisement for renting the upper floor of our home. Her words resonated with a hopeful tone, and I felt a glimmer of excitement. The prospect of having a family occupy the upper floor brought a sense of companionship, a balm for the solitude that had become a constant companion.

With anticipation in my voice, I invited Pallavi and her husband to visit the property the following morning. The connection we established through that simple phone call felt like a small yet significant step—a potential turning point in my journey towards reclaiming normalcy and companionship. As the conversation ended, a sense of purpose infused my actions, and I couldn't help but look forward to the meeting that awaited us.

As the next morning dawned, the anticipation of the new day's events swirled within me. The chime of the doorbell pulled me from my thoughts, and I hastened to open the door. There stood Pallavi, with her husband Ashish by her side, and two vibrant young girls named Meera and Divya, who were introduced to me as twin sisters of around 16 years old. Their presence instantly injected a sense of vitality into the atmosphere.

Pallavi's warm smile and the enthusiasm of her family was infectious, filling the space with an energy that had been absent for too long. It was heartening to see Meera and Divya's curiosity as they glanced around the house, their eyes alight with interest. Ashish's friendly demeanor and Pallavi's genuine conversation eased any initial awkwardness, as we discussed their requirements and preferences for the upper floor.

As we moved from room to room, I observed their reactions closely, hoping that they would find the space suitable for their needs. The girls' laughter resonated through the halls, and I felt a glimmer of hope that their presence could transform this house into a home once again. Amidst our conversation and exploration, the emptiness that had once pervaded the upper floor seemed to dissipate, replaced by the potential for a new beginning, a new connection.

Amid our explorations, Pallavi's meticulous eye for detail didn't go unnoticed. She assessed every nook and cranny, her fingers occasionally sweeping away a layer of dust as if envisioning the space in its full glory. Her concern about the condition of the rooms was palpable, and I found myself assuring her that I would ensure the upper floor was cleaned and prepared before their potential move-in. The thought of restoring the rooms, long forgotten and neglected, suddenly gained importance as her enthusiasm mirrored my own desire to rejuvenate the space.

The rent which i charged was very nominal, and even they happy as ashish business was in loss and they had to sell their house, for them it was a good deal, Ashish said, Okay so we like it and we will shift within a week. The satisfaction of finding a suitable family for the upper floor was immeasurable. Ashish's acceptance of the deal, his calm demeanor, and the excitement in Pallavi's eyes all affirmed my decision. As they expressed their intention to shift within a week, I felt a sense of gratification that extended beyond the financial aspect. Money had never been my primary concern, and knowing that the Deshmukh family would become part of my life brought me an unexpected sense of joy.

The satisfaction of finding a suitable family for the upper floor was immeasurable. Ashish's acceptance of the deal, his calm demeanor, and the excitement in Pallavi's eyes all affirmed my decision. As they expressed their intention to shift within a week, I felt a sense of gratification that extended beyond the financial aspect. Money had never been my primary concern, and knowing that the Deshmukh family would become part of my life brought me an unexpected sense of joy.

The arrival of the laborers and the bustling activity of cleaning the upper floor dispelled the lingering unease that had taken root in that space. Laxmi, our dependable house help, had gathered a team to make sure the place was spotless for the Deshmukh family's arrival. Their presence brought a renewed energy, transforming the once-neglected rooms into welcoming spaces. Chaya's visit added to the excitement; her happiness at the prospect of new companionship was evident, reflecting my own sentiments as well. The house, which had witnessed so much mystery and sorrow, was now being prepared to welcome a new chapter filled with hope and togetherness.

All this cleaning exercise took almost 3,4 days finally the cleaning crew left , it was 3 in the afternoon. I was very tired now that I was about to turn 60 .this level of exhaustion was indeed difficult for me, i sat on our sofa of living room and god knows when i slept there only while watching some serial on television

As I stirred awake, my surroundings felt unfamiliar and disorienting. The room was bathed in an eerie moonlight, casting elongated shadows across the floor. Confusion mingled with a creeping sense of dread as I struggled to recall how I had ended up here in the nursery. I had fallen asleep on the living room sofa, hadn't I? My heart raced, thudding loudly in my ears, drowning out the sounds of the night.

My mind raced to find a logical explanation, but my thoughts were clouded by an unsettling feeling that something was amiss. The shadows danced on the walls, and every creak of the old house seemed magnified, creating an unsettling symphony of sounds. I felt as if I was being watched, my every movement observed by unseen eyes.

A chill ran down my spine as I attempted to stand up, only to find my legs trembling beneath me. Was it exhaustion that had caused me to sleepwalk to this unfamiliar place? Or was there something more sinister at play? The events that had unfolded in this house over the years flooded my mind – the disappearances, the unexplained occurrences, the whispered rumours of a parallel world.

I mustered the courage to leave the room, my footsteps echoing through the empty corridor. The house felt different, transformed by the recent cleaning efforts, yet an undercurrent of unease remained. As I descended the staircase, a sense of foreboding tightened its grip on my heart. The once-familiar surroundings seemed foreign, each shadow concealing secrets and possibilities I couldn't comprehend.

With a trembling hand, I went near the nursery's door opened the door knob standing on the precipice of something I couldn't grasp.

And just like that I woke up, I was in my living room lying on sofa, sweating.so whatever i saw was that a dream? why it felt so real?

I sat up on the sofa, my heart still racing from the intensity of the dream—or was it more than that? The details were so vivid, the sensations so real that I found myself questioning the nature of reality itself. A cold sweat coated my skin, and a shiver traced its way down my spine.

Gazing around the living room, everything appeared as it should be. The familiar furniture, the soft glow of the lamp, and the comforting silence of my home. I took a deep breath, trying to steady my racing heart and clear my mind. It was just a dream, I reassured myself. Dreams can feel incredibly lifelike, stirring emotions that linger long after you wake up.

But the unease remained, a nagging feeling that I couldn't shake. It was as if a thin veil had been lifted, revealing a hidden layer of uncertainty beneath the surface of my reality. My rational mind fought to dismiss the dream as a product of an overactive imagination, yet a small voice within me whispered that there might be more to it.

I stood and walked around the living room, as if trying to anchor myself in the physical world. I touched the furniture, felt the texture of the cushions, and looked out of the window at the gentle moonlight bathing the surroundings. The world felt solid and real, but the dream's echo lingered like a shadow.

As I glanced at the mahogany table in the corner of the room, a flicker of the dream's candlelight seemed to dance at the edges of my memory. The sensation of being trapped, the weight on my chest, the chilling whisper—it all surged back into my consciousness. I shook my head, trying to banish the thoughts and regain my composure.

Turning on the lights, I walked to the kitchen and poured myself a glass of water. The cold liquid was soothing as it coursed down my throat, momentarily dispelling the remnants of the dream's unease. I stood by the kitchen window, looking out at the peaceful evening..

As I stood there, a sense of calm began to wash over me. Whether the dream had been a mere creation of my mind or something more profound, it was a reminder that the boundaries between reality and the unknown could sometimes blur. It prompted me to reflect on the mysteries of life, the unexplored corners of our experiences that we often dismiss or overlook.

With a determined exhale, I set the glass down and made my way back to the living room. The dream's lingering grip was fading, replaced by a renewed sense of resolve. Whatever it was that I had glimpsed in the dream, I was determined to face it head-on. Whether it was an exploration of my own fears and thoughts or a glimpse into something beyond, I was ready to embrace the journey ahead.

The soft light streamed through the windows as I prepared for the pooja, just as Sadh Guru Govind ji had advised. With a sense of purpose, I gathered fresh flowers from our garden, their vibrant colours a reflection of the beauty around me. Each blossom seemed to carry a touch of serenity and hope, reminding me of the simple joys that life could offer.

I immediately remembered what Sadh Guru Govind ji had told me to do, I need to perform pooja as per his guidance every morning and evening a Diya has to be lit in the house, I went to our garden picked some fresh flowers for pooja,

In the kitchen, I carefully selected sugar and a mix of dry fruits, arranging them in a small plate to offer as prasad. The rituals were a bridge to connect with the spiritual guidance I had received, a way to seek solace and clarity in the midst of my uncertainties. As I held the plate in my hands, a wave of gratitude washed over me—gratitude for the moments of reflection and the presence of mind to embrace them.

With the flowers and prasad ready, I made my way to the mandir. The gentle aroma of incense filled the air as I lit a Diya, its flickering flame casting a warm glow in the sacred space. I closed my eyes for a moment, taking a deep breath and allowing the serenity of the moment to envelop me.

As I began the pooja, the familiarity of the rituals brought a sense of comfort. I chanted a Shloka taught by my father, which we always used to chant while lighting diya in the evening which was

शुभं करोति कल्याणम् आरोग्यं धनसंपदा ।

शत्रुबुद्धिविनाशाय दीपज्योति नमोऽस्तुते ।

दविया दविया दपित्कार कानी कंुडले मोतीहार ।

दवियाला पाहून नमस्कार ॥१॥

दविा लावला देवापांशी, उजेड पडला तुळशीपांशी ।

माझा नमसकार सर्व देवापांशी ॥२॥

(I bow to the lamp of dawn/dusk whose light is supreme knowledge that dispels the darkness of ignorance and by which all can be achieved, Salutations to the light of the lamp, the originator of auspiciousness, health and prosperity, that destroys hostile feelings; Salutation to the light of that lamp.)

softly, my voice a mere whisper, as I offered the flowers and prasad to the divine. It felt as if I was not only performing the rituals but also reconnecting with a part of myself that had been lost amidst the chaos of life.

Memories of my baba performing pooja in our ancestral home flooded my mind. The scent of incense, the resonance of his chants, the feel of the cool marble floor—all of it came rushing back to me. In those moments, I felt a profound connection, a link between generations that transcended time itself.

As I concluded the pooja, a sense of peace settled within me. The diya continued to cast its gentle light, a symbol of the divine presence that had guided me to this moment. With Govind ji's words echoing in my mind, I took a deep breath and picked up the diya that flickered with the sacred flame from the mandir. The diya's warm glow seemed to infuse me with a sense of purpose and reassurance. I looked at the offering of prasad in my hand—the sugar and dry fruits—and felt a mix of anticipation and resolve.

As I ate a small bite of the prasad, a connection to the ritual formed. It was more than just consuming food; it was a symbolic act of communion with the divine, a reminder that the spiritual path I was embarking upon was a journey of both inner and outer transformation.

With the diya in one hand and the prasad in the other, I ascended the stairs to the upper floor, the scene of my vivid dream. The once-dusty space now felt charged with an eerie anticipation. My footsteps echoed in the corridor as I moved towards the room that had appeared so vividly in my sleep. The wooden door stood ajar, just as it had in the dream.

Despite my nervousness, I reminded myself of Govind ji's guidance—to face my fears and confront the unknown. I hesitated for a moment, the doorway seeming to be a threshold between reality and the inexplicable. Summoning my determination, I stepped forward and entered the room.

The mahogany table and chairs were just as I had seen in my dream, an eerie familiarity that sent shivers down my spine. The diya's light danced and flickered, casting intricate shadows on the walls. I placed the prasad on the table, a humble offering to whatever energies resided in this space.

With my heart racing, I positioned the diya next to the prasad. The flames seemed to waver, as if acknowledging the significance of the moment. As I stood there, I could almost sense a presence—a presence that was neither visible nor tangible, but one that seemed to linger in the air.

With a deep breath, I opened my eyes and turned to leave the room. As I stepped outside, a rush of emotions surged within me. The experience had been both unnerving and empowering, a collision of the known and the unknown. I held onto the diya, its flame now an embodiment of my resolve to navigate the mysteries that lay ahead.

As I descended the stairs, a sense of accomplishment washed over me. The ritual had been a step towards uncovering the truths that had remained hidden. With every passing day, I was discovering the depth of my strength, guided by the teachings of Sadh Guru Govind ji and my unwavering determination to confront the enigmas that had intertwined with my life.

As the clock struck 7:30 in the evening, a sense of unease clung to me like a shadow. The remnants of the day's thoughts still occupied my mind—the eerie dream, the ritual, and the unsettling atmosphere of the upper floor. Despite the fading light, I couldn't shake off the weight of the unusual experiences. My appetite had diminished, but I managed to push myself to consume a glass of milk, hoping it would bring some semblance of normalcy to the evening.

With the television on, I tried to divert my thoughts, but they kept drifting back to the events of the day. The minutes ticked by, and soon it was 9 PM—the hour I usually retired to bed. My eyes were heavy with sleep, and I made my way to the bedroom. The comfort of my bed welcomed me, and I closed my eyes, hoping for a peaceful night's rest.

However, the night turned out to be anything but peaceful. As I slept, the boundary between reality and dreams blurred, and I found myself immersed in a nightmarish vision. In this dream, sinister shadows seemed to dance and flicker around the diya—an unsettling sight that defied explanation. Hisses and whispers echoed in the darkness, as if something otherworldly was trying to reach out to the sacred flame. The diya's glow cast eerie, shifting patterns on the walls, intensifying the feeling of unease.

Suddenly, the sound of shattering glass shattered the dream's tension. The plate that held the prasad had fallen to the ground, its contents scattered across the floor. It was as if the dream's disturbing atmosphere had crossed over into reality, leaving me disoriented and alarmed. My eyes snapped open, my heart racing in my chest.

As I looked around the room, the morning light filtering through the curtains, I couldn't shake the feeling that something was amiss. Was it just a dream, or had there been an eerie presence in the room? The line between reality and the surreal had become indistinct, leaving me questioning the nature of my experiences. The unsettling night had left an imprint on me, a lingering unease that defied easy explanation.

A sense of trepidation gripped me as I rose from my bed to confront the aftermath of yesterday's ritual—an act I had undertaken as guided by Sadh guru Govind ji. The intention had been to gain insight into the nature of the battle I was about to face, and to ascertain if I was truly prepared for what lay ahead. My steps were hesitant as I made my way towards the upper floor, my heart beating faster with each passing moment.

The nursery room loomed ahead; its door slightly ajar. Swallowing my apprehension, I pushed the door open and entered, the scene that met my eyes sending a chill down my spine. The diya I had placed there had not only burnt out, but the oil it had contained seemed to have spilled in a circular pattern on the floor. The mitti diya, now in pieces, lay broken amidst the scattered remnants of burnt offerings. The prasad plate, once a delicate glass vessel, was now shattered into fragments, the dry fruits reduced to ashes.

The sight was disconcerting and surreal, as if the very elements of the ritual had been tampered with by an unseen force. The circle of spilled oil, the broken diya, and the shattered plate seemed to form a haunting tableau of disruption and chaos. Fear and uncertainty gnawed at me, mingling with the shock of the scene before me. The remnants of the ritual lay in disarray, their symbolic significance marred by a sense of malevolent intrusion.

As I stood there, grappling with the unsettling aftermath, I couldn't help but wonder if this was a sign—a sign that the battle ahead was not only real but also formidable. The confrontation with the unknown had begun, and the path ahead was fraught with uncertainty. The shattered diya and broken prasad plate seemed to symbolize the fragility of the barrier between realms, reminding me that the battle against the shadows was far from over.

The shattered remnants of the ritual lay before me, each piece seemingly imbued with its own significance. As I pondered the unsettling scene, it became evident that this act of sacredness had indeed disrupted the prevailing aura of darkness that had taken root within these walls. The spilled oil formed a circle, like a boundary crossed, a line that had been dared. The broken diya, a vessel that had contained the flame of hope, now lay fragmented—a stark reminder of the clash between light and shadow.

The prasad, intended as an offering to the divine, had become a conduit for divine energy, casting a light that pierced the veil of malevolence. It seemed as though this act of defiance, this intrusion into the realm of the sinister, had provoked a reaction. The shattered plate and burnt dry fruits hinted at the forceful rebuttal of a presence that refused to be vanquished easily.

A sense of trepidation and awe settled over me as I realized the implications of what had transpired. The very act that I had undertaken, guided by Govind Ji's counsel, had ignited a confrontation with an entity that thrived in the shadows. It was as if this place, devoid of sanctity for years, had been stirred from its slumber, provoked by the audacity of a single diya.

The words of Govind Ji echoed in my mind, resonating with a newfound significance. This ritual, a mere glimpse into the hidden truths that surrounded me, had offered more questions than answers. It had unveiled a realm of darkness that coexisted alongside our reality, a realm that my actions had threatened to breach.

The warning was clear, etched in the shattered fragments before me—a reminder that the journey ahead would be *fraught with challenges and perils beyond my comprehension. The battle was not just a physical one; it was a battle of energies, a clash of forces beyond the realm of ordinary understanding.*

As I stood amidst the aftermath of the unsettling events, a wave of doubt and uncertainty washed over me. Was I truly prepared to confront a malevolent force that defied the boundaries of my understanding? The shattered remnants of the ritual served as a stark reminder that this battle was unlike any I had encountered before. My heart sank as I grappled with the enormity of the challenge that lay ahead.

I couldn't deny the truth—I lacked the unwavering courage required to face such darkness head-on. My advancing age only added to the weight of my doubts. The thought of venturing into a realm where the lines between reality and the unknown blurred was intimidating, to say the least. The words of Govind Ji echoed in my mind, a reminder of the ominous path that loomed before me.

As I considered my options, I came to a difficult realization. Perhaps the battle that Govind Ji had alluded to wasn't meant for me. The circumstances that had led me to this point were extraordinary, and the forces at play seemed beyond my control. The mere thought of confronting an entity that thrived on malevolence was enough to send shivers down my spine.

Yet, as I grappled with my fears, another path emerged—one that didn't involve direct confrontation, but rather a pursuit of inner strength and spiritual grounding. Govind Ji's guidance had shown me the power of spirituality as a shield against the unknown. The rituals and practices he had recommended had offered a sense of solace and purpose, even in the face of uncertainty.

With a heavy heart, I realized that I might never meet Govind Ji again, at least not to embark on the battle he had hinted at. However, his teachings had left an indelible mark on me. The path of spirituality he had shown me became my refuge, a sanctuary against the terrors that lurked within the shadows. While I might not have the courage for the battle, I could fortify my spirit and find strength in the practices he had shared.

As the weight of the situation settled over me, I resolved to navigate this new chapter with the tools Govind Ji had provided. I would embrace the path of spirituality, seeking solace and protection in its rituals and wisdom. While the battle against darkness might remain beyond my grasp, the battle to cultivate inner strength and resilience was one that I could undertake with determination.

After a couple of days had passed since the unsettling incident, the Deshmukh family finally completed their move into the upper floor. They didn't bring much with them, a clear sign that this family had experienced their own share of hardships. It struck me that here I was, seeking companionship and a way to cope with my loneliness, while unknowingly benefitting from their presence. A pang of guilt tugged at my conscience, yet the yearning for connection outweighed my qualms.

As they settled in, arranging their belongings, Pallavi's attention was drawn to the locked nursery room. She inquired about it, expressing her hopes of providing separate rooms for her twin daughters, Meera and Divya. How could I explain the true nature of that room? Instead, I fabricated a reason, telling her that it held some old antiques that I didn't want to discard, resulting in its being locked. The girls' faces fell with disappointment, and I felt a twinge of remorse for having dampened their excitement.

In an effort to lift their spirits, I decided to make a hearty Pav Bhaji for dinner that evening. We all gathered around the table and shared a meal together, and in that moment, it felt as if we were a genuine family. The laughter, the chatter, and the sense of togetherness were immensely gratifying to me. Amidst the challenges and mysteries that shrouded my life, these simple moments of connection became my source of comfort and joy.

As two more days drifted by, Pallavi worked tirelessly to arrange the upper floor to her liking. She transformed the space into a cozy haven, dividing it into a bedroom and a small kitchen. Her daughters, Divya and Meera, shared a room, and she even brought in a small Ganesha idol that she placed in the lobby area. It was a heartwarming sight to see her setting up her own rituals and starting anew within the house. Her devotion was evident when I noticed her performing a pooja for the first time in that very place.

Pallavi's small act of faith felt like a beacon of hope in the midst of my own fears and uncertainties. Although I was still conflicted about the power of the evil that seemed to linger, I realized that whatever malevolent force was at play, it was connected to me and not to this family. As I contemplated the prasad she had brought down to offer me, Pallavi's voice broke through the silence. She asked if I was okay, concern in her eyes. I managed a reassuring smile and nodded, asking if she needed anything.

With genuine warmth, she revealed that it was their wedding anniversary that day. They had decided to invite a few friends for a small get-together, and Pallavi had planned a pooja to mark the occasion. I congratulated her on the anniversary and offered my best wishes. To lend a helping hand, I sent Laxmi to assist her in the kitchen. Wanting to extend a gesture of celebration, I also ordered some sweets as a gift for the couple. In that moment, despite the undercurrent of fear and mystery in my life, I found solace in the simple joys of sharing in others' happiness.

As the evening sun began to set, the Deshmukh family's wedding anniversary celebration commenced around 6 PM. Around 15 people gathered for the auspicious pooja and the subsequent get-together. It was an atmosphere that hadn't graced the upper floor in decades, and the sense of togetherness felt reassuring amidst the lingering mysteries.

The pooja, a harmonious blend of tradition and modernity, concluded by 9 PM, and the delightful aroma of dinner filled the air. Guests enjoyed the spread of dishes and mingled with one another. By the time it was 9:30, the upper floor was bustling with laughter and conversation, bringing life to a space that had been dormant for so long.

Around 9:45, I returned to my room, my heart warmed by the familial atmosphere. I performed my regular pooja at our home's mandir, seeking solace and protection in my rituals. As the clock approached 11 PM, the guests began to bid their farewells after a cake-cutting ceremony. The house gradually quietened, and by 12 AM, the night had settled into a stillness.

However, just as I was drifting into sleep, a sudden, ear-piercing scream shattered the silence. The shriek was so intense that it jolted me awake, my heart pounding with apprehension. The scream persisted for what felt like an eternity, a chilling sound that seemed to reverberate through the entire house. It was unmistakably coming from Divya and Meera's room.

Panic spread through me as I tried to comprehend the source of the terror. The next few minutes were a blur of hurried footsteps, frantic activity, and the girls' voices in distress. The commotion went on for about 15 minutes before an eerie stillness settled in once more. With a mix of concern and confusion, I eventually allowed myself to believe that it must have been an intense argument between the sisters, although the intensity of the scream had been unlike anything I'd ever heard.

I lay back down, attempting to put my racing thoughts to rest and attributing the incident to mere teenage drama. Despite my efforts, sleep remained elusive, and I pondered the strange occurrences that had unfolded within the walls of Shanti Villa.

The night had been a long and restless one, my mind haunted by the piercing scream that had shattered the tranquillity of the upper floor. Sleep eluded me as I lay in my bed, my thoughts racing and my senses on high alert. The urge to rush upstairs and investigate was strong, but the fear of intruding on their privacy held me back. Instead, I tossed and turned, anxiously awaiting the morning light.

As the first rays of sunlight filtered into my room, I wasted no time in getting out of bed. An unsettling feeling gnawed at me, urging me to go upstairs and ensure that everything was alright. Stepping out of my room and into the living area, I was met with a scene that both surprised and puzzled me.

There, on the couch and scattered around the floor, lay Ashish, Pallavi, Divya, and Meera, all sound asleep. The family had spent the night in the living area, huddled together as if seeking comfort and safety. Divya and Meera clung to their mother, their faces peaceful in slumber, their expressions far removed from the terror of the previous night's scream.

My heart softened at the sight, understanding that their actions were perhaps a response to something much deeper than mere teenage squabbles. They had sought solace and togetherness, a united front against the unknown forces that had unsettled the upper floor.

My footsteps in the morning hush had stirred Pallavi and Ashish from their sleep. Their faces were drained of colour, their eyes wide with a mixture of fear and exhaustion. I approached them cautiously, sensing their unease, and gently inquired about the previous night's events.

"Pallavi, Ashish, what happened?" I asked, my voice carrying a mixture of concern and confusion. "I heard some screams in the night. Are you both alright? And why are you sleeping out here like this?"

Pallavi's voice trembled as she began to recount the unsettling events. "Aunty, after dinner, Ashish and I went to see our friends off at the gate," she explained wearily. "I asked Meera and Divya to get ready for bed as it was nearly midnight. But as they were about to go to their room, they saw that the nursery room's door was wide open. There was a faint, eerie light spilling out from within."

I listened intently, my heart quickening with a mixture of anticipation and dread. Pallavi continued after a moment's pause, her voice quivering. "Meera and Divya were curious and ventured inside the room. And there, Aunty... there they saw..." Pallavi faltered, her words catching in her throat. She took a deep breath, gathering herself to continue. "There they saw three figures sitting on those chairs, swaying back and forth in a rhythmic motion."

My blood ran cold at Pallavi's words, my mind racing to comprehend the gravity of what she was describing. The image of those figures, sitting in the dimly lit room and moving with a disturbing rhythm, etched itself into my mind. Meera's shock was so profound that she couldn't even speak, leaving Divya to recount the eerie encounter.

As the truth of their experience settled over me, a chilling realization gripped my heart. The darkness that had haunted the upper floor had not relented; it had taken on a more sinister and tangible form. The realms of the unknown had intersected with the lives of this family, leaving them shaken and vulnerable.

My footsteps in the morning hush had stirred Pallavi and Ashish from their sleep. Their faces were drained of color, their eyes wide with a mixture of fear and exhaustion. I approached them cautiously, sensing their unease, and gently inquired about the previous night's events.between reality and the inexplicable blurred further, leaving us with more questions than answers.

As Pallavi's voice quivered with anxiety, she continued to recount the unsettling events of the previous night. "And, Aunty, when Ashish and I were ascending the stairs, both Meera and Divya came running to us," she said, her eyes reflecting the lingering fear. "Divya, who was utterly terrified, asked us what had happened. Me and Ashish were alarmed, so we immediately rushed to check the room."

My heart raced as I listened, hanging onto every word. Pallavi's account painted a picture of escalating tension and unexplainable phenomena. "The room was still open," she continued, her voice a mix of apprehension and disbelief, "but as Ashish and I attempted to enter, the door slammed shut right in front of us. We tried to open it, but it remained stubbornly shut. Frustrated and unnerved, we eventually gave up and retreated. We had no choice but to sleep downstairs, as we didn't dare to stay on the upper floor."

The weight of their experience pressed down on me, its implications reverberating through my thoughts. The upper floor, once a haven of mystery, had transformed into a place of undeniable malevolence. The veil between the worlds had thinned, and the barriers that separated the unknown from the known had been breached.

I exchanged a look with Ashish, sensing the distress and bewilderment that gripped him. The events of that night were beyond rational explanation, and the sense of powerlessness in the face of the inexplicable was palpable.

As the realization of their plight settled in, a sense of responsibility mingled with my concern. I understood that my role in this unfolding drama was far from over. The forces at play were beyond ordinary comprehension, and the battle against the unknown had become a fight for survival, for protection, and perhaps for redemption.

As Pallavi, Ashish, and I exchanged perplexed glances, we suddenly noticed that Meera and Divya were wide awake, their gaze fixed intently on a wall in front of them. It was as if their attention was drawn to something we couldn't perceive. Pallavi's voice quivered as she addressed her daughters, her words laden with fear, "Mamma, these two were there yesterday... but they looked so different. Like one-dimensional figures, just flat faces and paper-like bodies." Her voice trembled as she spoke, and her eyes widened with a mixture of disbelief and terror.

Confusion clouded our minds as we followed her gaze to the wall they were staring at. And then it hit us with chilling clarity—the Two photo frames on the wall. I could feel my heart racing as I comprehended what they were implying. Meera and Divya had seen something... something that defied all reason and reality.

Their young voices quivered as they continued to describe the unfathomable sight they had witnessed. "They were there," Meera said, her voice trembling like a leaf in the wind. "Ma and Dada, but not like the photos we know. They were like flat shapes, as if drawn on paper."

My mind reeled as I connected the dots. The three figures they saw—the two-dimensional figures—were, according to them, Alok's parents. The very ones who had vanished from this house, leaving a legacy of mystery and fear.

Driven by a need to understand, I dashed to my room and retrieved an old album containing our family photographs. With a photo clutched in my hand, I returned to the room and held it before Divya's gaze. Her eyes widened, and she let out a horrified scream, "He was the third one!"

I felt the ground shift beneath me as I collapsed onto the floor, grappling with the magnitude of what I had just heard and seen. Alok's photo—the third figure they saw. It was inconceivable, yet the evidence was right before us.

The dimensions of reality seemed to warp and twist, merging the past and present in a haunting tableau. The once-unseen forces lurking within this house had shattered the boundaries of time and existence, revealing a terrifying tableau of figures that should have remained forever beyond our comprehension.

As the weight of the situation settled in, I was consumed by a sense of foreboding dread. The events of the past night had opened a Pandora's box of unsettling questions, each more terrifying than the last. What sinister force had been unleashed by the simple act of arranging a small pooja and welcoming Deshmukh family into our home? Was their positivity and light somehow a catalyst for the malevolent energies that seemed to have taken root within our walls?

My mind raced with chilling possibilities. Could it be that the evil entities that had been lying dormant for years were now stirred by the introduction of sanctity? Was their realm one that reacted violently to any intrusion, protecting itself from the purity and goodness that now resided here? And what of my own missing family – had they become enmeshed in this sinister web as well?

The weight of guilt bore heavily on me. Deshmukh family had come here with hopes of a fresh start, seeking solace and companionship. The realization that their positivity had somehow ignited a malevolent response was a thought too dreadful to bear. It was as if their happiness was an affront to the evil that lurked, and they were now paying the price for it. The house seemed to take on an even darker atmosphere. The air was heavy with the unknown, and every corner held a sense of trepidation. The boundary between reality and the supernatural was growing thinner by the day, and the answers I so desperately sought remained elusive. What was the connection between the missing figures, the eerie occurrences, and the evil forces that now seemed to permeate our home?

I realized that the battle I was facing was not just against the physical manifestations of evil, but against forces that transcended our world. The lines between good and evil, past and present, had blurred in ways that defied comprehension. And amid this turmoil, I couldn't escape the lingering fear that my own missing family – Ma, Dada, and Alok – were somehow entangled in this nightmare, their presence felt even in their absence.

As darkness settled over the house, I couldn't help but feel a sense of helplessness. The evil that had been roused was beyond my understanding, and the consequences of our actions had taken a nightmarish turn. The Deshmukh family's arrival had unknowingly disrupted a balance that was centuries old, plunging us all into a realm of horror that defied explanation. And as I stood amidst the shadows, I couldn't shake the feeling that we were all mere pawns in a much larger, malevolent game – a game that threatened to consume us all.

The memories of my father's tragic demise rushed back, intertwining with the current turmoil that had gripped our house. The image of him lying lifeless on the upper floor, clutching his pooja book with a look of terror frozen in his open eyes, etched itself into my mind. Had he too encountered the malevolent presence that seemed to lurk in the shadows? Could his spiritual devotion have inadvertently brought him face to face with something so vile?

As these thoughts swirled within me, I couldn't shake the fear that Deshmukh family might also fall prey to the same sinister forces that had claimed my family members. I couldn't bear the thought of those innocent girls, Divya and Meera, becoming ensnared in a web of darkness beyond their understanding. The echoes of their screams from the previous night reverberated in my ears, a haunting reminder of the malevolence that lingered.

The Deshmukh family had stepped into this house seeking a fresh start, oblivious to the haunting history that lay hidden within its walls. They deserved a life free from the taint of evil, a chance to rebuild their happiness without the burden of supernatural dread. It was my responsibility to protect them, to shield them from the horrors that had plagued my own family.

As much as I valued their companionship and the solace, they had brought me, I knew that they needed to leave. The risk was too great, the consequences too dire. The safety and well-being of Divya and Meera had to take precedence, and I couldn't afford to gamble with their lives. I had to ensure that they didn't become another chapter in the sinister history that this house held.

With a heavy heart, I made the difficult decision to ask the Deshmukh family to move on. It wasn't a decision I took lightly, but it was a necessary one. They deserved to find happiness without the looming spectre of evil overshadowing their lives. As I steeled myself to have this conversation, I couldn't shake the feeling that I was on the precipice of a battle much larger than myself – a battle that spanned generations and dimensions, a battle against the very essence of darkness itself.

The decision to ask the Deshmukh family to leave weighed heavily on my heart, but I knew it was the right choice. Their safety and well-being were my utmost priority, and I couldn't bear the thought of them facing the same horrors that my family had endured. The days that followed their departure were filled with a profound sense of emptiness. The once-lively house had fallen back into its quiet, desolate state.

For two weeks, Shanti Villa seemed to regain a semblance of normalcy. The absence of Divya and Meera's laughter and the warmth of their presence left an ache in my heart. The house felt lonelier than ever, as if it too mourned the departure of the family that had briefly brought light to its shadowed corners.

Despite the solitude, a sense of unease still lingered in the air. The memory of the eerie figures and the unsettling events of that fateful night refused to fade. I found myself haunted by questions that had no answers – what had triggered those malevolent manifestations? Was it the result of the sacred rituals I had performed? Or was it a warning against any intrusion into the dark dimensions that existed within the house?

I realized that the battle against this supernatural force was far from over. The evil that had plagued this house for generations was still very much a part of its fabric, and I couldn't ignore the fact that my own missing family members seemed to be connected to it. The unsettling feeling persisted, like a storm brewing on the horizon.

As I walked through the now-empty rooms, memories of the Deshmukh family's brief stay echoed in the corners of my mind. Their departure had left a void, a stark reminder of the fragility of companionship and the ever-present undercurrent of darkness that enveloped Shanti Villa. I knew that I had to face the truth – the battle against this malevolent force was mine to fight, and I couldn't shy away from the responsibility that had been thrust upon me. The house may have returned to its quiet state, but the looming threat still lingered, waiting for the right moment to strike again.

In my pursuit of finding solace and distancing myself from the horrors that had unfolded, I decided to take drastic measures. The upper floor had become a realm of fear and darkness, and I was determined to sever any connection between it and the ground floor. I summoned workers and contractors to undertake the task, conveying my urgency to complete the work within a span of just a few days.

A massive, imposing wooden door was crafted, its sheer presence an eerie reminder of the divide it was meant to create. As it was installed, I couldn't help but feel a sense of unease—a heavy barrier between the two levels of the house, symbolizing the chasm between my reality and the malevolent forces that had haunted the upper floor.

To ensure the security of this new separation, a large metal lock was brought in. It was a formidable addition, promising to keep the door locked and secure, safeguarding me from the malevolence that had once crossed the threshold. With each heavy clang of the lock, I hoped to banish the unsettling memories that had haunted me for so long.

Yet, in my naivety, I failed to realize that such a simple physical barrier could not erase the supernatural bond that had formed. As I stood before the newly fortified door, I couldn't shake off the feeling that I was merely putting a bandage on a wound that ran far deeper. The true connection, it seemed, was not bound by locks and doors, but by something far more sinister and inexplicable.

A few days later, a letter arrived inviting me to a Yoga and Meditation program in Lonavala, organized by the club that Alok and I had joined. Being a lifetime member, I received this invitation, and I saw it as a chance to take a break from the unsettling events in the house. Lonavala seemed like a distant oasis of tranquility, a respite from the looming shadows of Shanti Villa. As evening fell, Chhaya visited for our customary tea. I chose not to divulge the details of the Deshmukh family's departure, wanting to avoid any potential gossip or unwelcome discussions.

Chhaya, always a source of comfort and wisdom, encouraged me to embrace this opportunity for a small trip. She believed it could offer a positive experience and a chance to rejuvenate my spirit. After contemplating her words, I made the decision to go on the trip. Four days later, I boarded the luxury bus arranged by the club, slowly getting acquainted with the other members onboard. The sense of moving away from Shanti Villa and its haunting memories brought a profound relief, like shedding a heavy burden that had rested on my shoulders.

As the journey progressed, I found myself surrounded by friendly faces, engaging in conversations and experiencing moments of genuine laughter. The weight that had accompanied me for so long began to lighten, and I could feel a glimmer of hope returning. Lonavala's serene landscapes and the company of fellow travellers gave me a sense of liberation from the clutches of the past. During those days, I found solace in the practice of yoga and meditation, reconnecting with my inner self and finding a measure of tranquillity that had been missing for far too long.

During my time away, a decision took shape in my mind. The experience made me realize that Shanti Villa, with its history and darkness, had taken a toll on me. I resolved that selling the property and moving somewhere nearby was the right course of action. The fear of meeting the same fate as Ma,Dada and Alok was deeply ingrained, and I was determined to break free from the cycle of tragedy that seemed to surround the house. As I returned from the trip, a renewed sense of determination propelled me forward, ready to confront my demons and make a change for the better.

On the third day of our meditation program, we were gathered in the expansive lawn of the hotel property, surrounded by the majestic mountains and lush trees. The serene setting seemed like the perfect backdrop for our deep meditation practice. Under the guidance of our coach, I closed my eyes and delved into the meditative state, seeking inner peace and calm.

When I opened my eyes, a profound disorientation swept over me. I found myself standing at the very door of the nursery room on the upper floor of Shanti Villa. A chill raced down my spine as I saw them—the dreaded figures that Divya had described—lifeless, white, one-dimensional shapes that moved with an eerie fluidity. It was as if I was staring at living paper cutouts, a macabre sight that seemed impossible to be real.

My legs were paralyzed, refusing to obey my commands. Panic surged through me, and I desperately searched for the staircase that should have led me downstairs, but it wasn't there. Was I trapped here? The figures seemed to be beckoning me, and among them stood Alok, or at least someone who looked like him. His gesture indicated that I should join them in the room. As if compelled by some unseen force, I found myself stepping closer, my body moving against my will. My eyes widened with horror as I noticed a fourth chair beside the others – as though they were waiting for me to join them.

A guttural scream escaped my lips, piercing through the eerie silence. Suddenly, I was jolted back to reality by the voice of our meditation coach, gently bringing me out of my deep meditation. The tranquil hotel surroundings flooded back into view, and the feeling of dread began to fade. Was it all just a vivid dream? Had the meditation process inadvertently transported me back to Shanti Villa, or was it something more sinister – a suggestion that these malevolent entities could follow me, no matter where I went?

Questions and uncertainty swirled around me, leaving me shaken and overwhelmed. Was this my fate now – to be forever haunted by these inexplicable forces? The experience left me rattled, further entwining me in the enigmatic web that seemed to connect my past, the present, and an ominous future.

The coach skillfully managed to diffuse the situation, attributing my experience to the depths of meditation. Though I felt embarrassed by the curious glances of others, I tried to compose myself. After the session, we all proceeded to the hotel restaurant where a sumptuous lunch awaited us. Finding a table, I focused on my meal, attempting to shake off the unsettling memories of the meditation.

However, my unease resurfaced when I noticed a familiar sight in the corner of the restaurant—a mahogany table and four chairs, the same as the one from the upper floor of Shanti Villa. My heart raced, and a sense of discomfort overcame me. I managed to finish my lunch hastily and made a swift retreat to my hotel room.

Hours passed as I stayed cooped up in my room, seeking refuge in television shows. The hunger eventually drove me to the restaurant for dinner. But as I settled down at my table, my gaze was inexplicably drawn to the very same table, now occupied by the three figures that had haunted me. Alok's eerie smile sent shivers down my spine, and I felt an ominous pull, as if he was beckoning me to join them.

The shock of it all was too much to bear. I abandoned my meal and fled back to my room, overcome by panic. I urgently contacted the club manager, fabricating an excuse about being unwell, pleading for my return journey to be arranged. I knew I needed to leave, to escape the relentless grip of these entities. It became clear that they were sending me a warning: come back home, or face their haunting presence, possibly with dire consequences for those around me.

With a heavy heart, I left the peaceful retreat and returned to Shanti Villa, succumbing to the inescapable truth that I was tethered to this place, and these entities, no matter how terrifying, were now a part of my life.

As days turned into nights, and the haunting presence of those entities persisted, I came to a stark realization—I was inextricably bound to this house, to the history it held, to the sins that had been committed under its roof. How could I escape a fate that seemed so intricately intertwined with my own existence? The luxury and comfort I had enjoyed all these years were built upon a foundation tainted by the suffering and dreams of innocent lives.

It was no longer possible to ignore the truth that I had conveniently distanced myself from the dark deeds that had paved the way for the grandeur I now lived in. I had overlooked the fact that the wealth and luxury I had come to cherish were the result of the misfortune and greed that had cost Alok's father and my dada their morality and compassion.

As the weight of my actions and the shadows of the past loomed larger, I couldn't escape the undeniable reality of karma. How could I absolve myself from the bad karma that had been accumulated over time? I had lived a life of privilege, reveling in the material comforts while turning a blind eye to the pain and suffering that had fueled it.

With a heavy heart, I faced the truth that I couldn't simply escape the consequences of my actions. I accepted my fate, acknowledging the karmic debt that tied me to this house, to these malevolent entities. I made a conscious decision to live with this haunting reality until the end of my days, knowing that I couldn't undo the past but could perhaps find a way to mitigate the darkness that had taken root. My life was now entwined with the history and the haunting, and I would bear the burden until my journey reached its inevitable conclusion.

As I sit down to pen these final words in this diary, I am overwhelmed by a sense of urgency and the need to record the truth for whoever comes to possess this house in the future. These days, my once-structured routine is in shambles, a casualty of the relentless grip that the entities within these walls have on my mind. The simple act of remembering if I've performed my daily pooja has become a challenge, a testament to the extent to which they are now toying with my sanity.

For years, the shield of spirituality that Sadhguru Govind ji introduced me to has been my refuge, a guiding light in the darkness that befell Shanti Villa after Alok's disappearance. Yet, even that sanctuary is slipping through my grasp, a cruel testament to the strength of the forces that now consume me. The entities have become more than just a presence; they are now active participants in my thoughts, a menacing presence that threatens to unravel whatever semblance of normalcy I've clung to.

I've come to realize that these entities, these manifestations of evil, have insidiously penetrated every aspect of this house. They've stripped away my sense of control, reduced me to a mere pawn in their twisted game. The spiritual path I embraced after Alok's vanishing has been my anchor, and now, as I lose my grip on it, I find myself spiraling further into the abyss.

I can feel it—the end approaching, the culmination of all these years of fear and uncertainty. I know that my time is limited, that my fate is intertwined with the malevolence that has plagued this place. This diary is my final attempt to document the horrors that have unfolded within these walls, to provide a glimpse into the darkness that exists beyond the surface. May whoever reads these words be prepared for the battles that lie ahead, for the connections that are stronger than any physical barrier.

As I write these closing lines, a haunting realization settles over me—I am becoming a part of the very history I've chronicled, a victim of the sinister forces that have made Shanti Villa their home. My days are numbered, and while I may never know the full truth, I can only hope that my words serve as a cautionary tale to those who dare to step into this world of malevolent shadows.

CHAPTER SIX

A Journey into the Unknown

As the first light of dawn peeked through the window of his apartment, Deven sat back in his chair, the weight of the diary's revelations settling heavily on his mind. He had spent the entire night engrossed in the pages that recounted the haunting history of Shanti Villa. A mixture of curiosity, fascination, and a newfound connection with Mrs. Asha Joshi had driven him to delve into this enigma. The lines between his own life and the unsettling narrative within the diary were blurring, and he couldn't ignore the call to action.

He contemplated the course of action he should take. Many would have chosen to capitalize on the situation, to sell the property and reap its financial benefits. However, Deven wasn't like most people. He had always been a solitary individual, disconnected from the world around him. But something about Mrs. Asha Joshi's story had resonated with him deeply. It wasn't just a story of malevolent forces and supernatural occurrences—it was a tale of struggle, tragedy, and the quest for understanding.

Mrs. Joshi had lived a life marred by fear and loneliness, haunted by the inexplicable events that had taken place in Shanti Villa. Deven felt a sense of empathy for her, a desire to uncover the truth that lay hidden beneath the layers of mystery. He couldn't just turn a blind eye and walk away from her plight. Instead, he felt compelled to confront the forces that had cast their shadow over her life and the lives of those who had come before her.

Determined, Deven considered his next steps. He realized that solving the puzzle of Shanti Villa wouldn't be easy, and the risks were considerable. Yet, he was driven by a newfound purpose, a need to bring closure to a story that had been left untold for too long. As the morning sun bathed his apartment in gentle light, Deven made up his mind. He would embark on a journey to uncover the truth, to face the malevolence that had plagued Shanti Villa, and to stand alongside Mrs. Asha Joshi in her battle against the forces of darkness.

Deven's mind was racing with plans and possibilities as he contemplated his next moves in the unfolding mystery of Shanti Villa. Three key figures stood out in his quest for answers.

First on his list was Dr. Manish Rathi, the psychologist whom Alok Joshi had consulted. Deven believed that Dr. Rathi might have insights into the psychological aspects of the haunting and the experiences shared by Mrs. Asha Joshi. A quick internet search yielded the doctor's contact information, and Deven promptly booked an appointment for the evening at 5.

Next was Govind Ji, the spiritual guide whose teachings Mrs. Asha Joshi had followed. Deven sensed that Govind Ji possessed knowledge about the paranormal events that had plagued Shanti Villa. He wanted to explore the spiritual angle and understand if there was a deeper significance to these occurrences.

The third person on his list was Mrs. Chaya Pathak, the neighbor who had inquired about Mrs. Asha Joshi's well-being. Deven recalled her invitation to visit her house, and he believed that she might have information about the whereabouts of Govind Ji. Perhaps she could provide insights into the spiritual practices followed by Mrs. Asha and the role they played in the haunting.

Deven had decided to return to Shanti Villa in the morning, not as a mere visitor but as an investigator with a mission. The property, once seen as an inherited asset, now held a deeper significance. It was a place shrouded in mystery, a site of tragedy and malevolent forces. Deven felt a sense of responsibility to unearth the truth, to bring justice to the woman who had lived in fear for years, and to confront the dark forces that had claimed numerous lives within those walls. Shanti Villa was no longer just bricks and walls to him; it was a place of history and haunting, and Deven was determined to uncover its secrets.

Deven was resolute in his decision to uncover the mysteries of Shanti Villa. He had taken the necessary steps to free up his schedule and focus entirely on this daunting task. With his leave request submitted and approved, he had a clear path ahead.

After a refreshing shower and a simple breakfast, Deven was ready to embark on his journey once more. He booked an Uber to Shanti Villa, the place that had both terrified and intrigued him. Despite the fear and uncertainty, he had felt on his previous visit, today, he was armed with determination and a burning curiosity to face whatever lay ahead.

As the car pulled up to Shanti Villa, Deven took a deep breath. He knew that this investigation would take him deeper into the unknown, but he was prepared to go to great lengths to uncover the truth and bring justice to those affected by the malevolent forces that had plagued this house for far too long.

Deven's second visit to Shanti Villa was marked by a stark contrast in his emotions. The grandeur that had awed him before was now overshadowed by a profound sense of unease. He entered the premises, passing the charming canopy where he imagined Mrs. Asha Joshi and his father had once sat during their initial visit, where her marriage got fixed, and her journey in this house began.

As he approached the main gate of the house. As he entered to his left was locked door leading to the upper floor, he now understood why it had been secured. After crossing the lobby Inside, he was now at the living room where the Deshmukh family had sought refuge from the haunting upper floor. The photo frames of Mr. Shanti Devi and Mr. Anand, Mrs. Asha's in-laws, stood as a reminder of the incident Divya had described to the family.

Deven continued his search, making his way to Mr. Alok's study room, hoping to find the medical records of Mr.Alok, he needed for Dr. Manish Rathi. After some thorough searching, he located the file he sought and also discovered a phone book with Mrs. Asha's contacts, including Mrs. Chaya Pathak's number.He saved it immediately in his cell phone.

Now, he faced the daunting task of venturing into the upper floor, the epicenter of eerie occurrences. Deven had to confront his fear, for if he couldn't overcome this initial hurdle, he wouldn't be equipped for the challenges ahead. Unlocking the metal door with a key, he ascended the stairs, his mind filled with the stories of Mrs. Asha's visits and her eerie experiences.

At entrance of the upper floor, he saw a room which Mrs. Asha's father must be using, Deshmukh family also had a small stay here and Divya and Meera had encountered something eerie there, Deven found himself standing in front of the nursery room, where supposedly that crooked evil figures if Shanti Devi Anand Ji & Alok's were found sitting at that the bizarre table and chairs. The eerie handprints and marks were still visible, and this time they were clearer than yesterday as if few hours ago some gathering has happened here. yesterday while going home, he saw a shadow from this room only as he could see the main entry gate from there where he was standing waiting for the Uber, had something otherworldly been watching him from this very room? is Mrs. Asha here somewhere? A sense of unease washed over him; He decided to retreat for now.

Next, he approached the attic, where more eerie marks of footprints and handprints, as well as a trail of something being dragged, were evident. Deven hesitated at the door but couldn't muster the courage to enter. He locked the attic door securely, clutching the keys, and then dialled Mrs. Chaya Pathak's number, hoping she could provide some information about

Sadh Guru Govind Ji.

Deven dialed Mrs. Chaya Pathak's number, his anticipation building as the phone rang. After a few moments, a lady's voice answered, "Hello?"

"Hello, this is Deven Kulkarni," he began. "I wanted to talk to Mrs. Chaya Pathak."

"Deven Kulkarni?" There was a brief pause before the lady continued, her voice softening. "Oh, yes, yes, Deven Beta. Now I recollected. How are you? And how did you get my number?"

Deven explained that he had found Mrs. Asha Joshi's phone diary, which contained her contact information. He then made his request: "I wanted to meet you for five minutes, Aunty. This is important. I am at Shanti Villa right now. I know your house. Can I come over?"

"Of course, Beta," Mrs. Pathak replied warmly. "I am at home. Please come over. I am waiting for you."

With that, they hung up, and Deven, clutching the medical records, locked the door behind him and made his way to the neighbouring building where Mrs. Pathak resided.

Deven reached Mrs. Chaya Pathak's house and rang the doorbell. She opened the door and welcomed him with a warm smile, inviting him inside. They sat on a sofa, and her husband, Mr. Ketan, joined them, his curiosity evident about Deven's sudden visit. After some casual conversation about the weather and politics, Deven decided to get to the point.

He began, "I don't want to take up too much of your time, but as I was reading Mrs. Asha's diary, I came across a mention that after her husband's sudden disappearance, you both took her to a satsang."

Mrs. Chaya nodded, her expression becoming thoughtful. "Yes, we did. She was going through a very dark phase in her life, and we thought she needed a distraction. She even asked some questions during the satsang. But after that day, whenever I approached her to join us again, she declined. That was almost 7-8 years ago."

Deven replied, "Yes, I know. I just needed to know if you have any address or contact number for that place. Are you still in touch with it?"

Mrs. Pathak answered, "Once a person finds solace in spirituality, it becomes like an addiction. Yes, we still go there once a month. The address is still the same, and Govind Ji has developed the place quite nicely. I'll share the address with you."

Deven felt a sense of relief as he received the address. This was another step on his journey to uncover the truth. He thanked the couple and said his goodbyes pleasantly, ready to take the next step in his investigation.

It was nearly 5 o'clock, and Deven had booked an appointment with Dr. Rathi under the guise of a patient. He had taken some photos of the family from the photo album he found in Mrs. Asha's bedroom, which he carried on his cellphone. Patiently, he waited in the lobby until his name was called.

Dr. Rathi's office was soothing, with light and pleasant colours, adorned with numerous plants that contributed to the overall positive atmosphere one would expect in a psychologist's clinic. Dr. Rathi, a man in his 60s, motioned for Deven to sit on a couch across from him. He took out his notepad and asked, "So, Deven, tell me, how can I help you?"

Deven began, "First of all, Doctor, I'd like to apologize for meeting you like this. I'm not a patient here. Actually, I have a few questions about your previous patient, Mr. Alok Joshi. Here's his file with records and the medicines you prescribed for him. I'm a relative, and I've recently acquired their house."

Dr. Rathi's face remained expressionless, but his displeasure at Deven's approach was evident. "Mr. Deven, first and foremost, this is not acceptable. As a doctor, I am not allowed to discuss my patients with strangers. It's a matter of confidentiality and their privacy. Please leave."

Deven, understanding the doctor's position, continued earnestly, "I completely understand, Doctor, and I respect your every word. But some strange things have happened in that house. Mr. Alok's wife, Mrs. Asha, disappeared in the exact same way Mr. Alok did. She had some bad experiences in the house, much like seeing her in-laws and Alok on the upper floor in an eerie way after their disappearances. She started losing herself, as she couldn't distinguish between what's real and what's a dream. Did something similar happen to Alok? I really need to know. Both of them deserve closure. Please, Doctor, I truly need your help here."

Deven maintained eye contact with the doctor, recognizing that he was an expert at reading people's faces and minds. Perhaps the doctor sensed the sincerity in Deven's approach. Dr. Rathi asked Deven to hand over the medical files, and Deven willingly complied, also showing Mr. Alok's photo to the doctor.

Dr. Rathi examined the file and the photo for a while, then went to his laptop, where he likely stored his patients' data digitally. Deven waited patiently for about 15 minutes, his curiosity building.

When Dr. Rathi returned to his seat, he fixed his sharp gaze on Deven and began to speak. "Well, Deven, Mr. Alok was indeed going through a period of severe mental distress. It started with him hearing voices in the night, sounds of someone running and thudding on the upper floor. However, as per his account, no one lived up there. With time, his condition deteriorated further. He began seeing his lost and missing parents randomly in the house, but not in the way a son would expect to see his parents. These were more like ghostly images, as he described them. No medication seemed to alleviate his suffering."

Dr. Rathi continued, "My analysis suggested that this condition may have had a genetic component, as his mother had also experienced similar hallucinations. It seemed that the consecutive losses of his parents in such tragic ways had a profound impact on him. During his last few sessions, he mentioned that he used to sleep in his study but would wake up on the upper floor in the middle of the night. This, understandably, terrified him. Deven listened attentively as Dr. Rathi continued to share his insights. "See, Deven," the doctor said, "our subconscious mind is a fascinating realm where creativity and imagination often run wild. It has a remarkable ability to conjure up ideas, images, and stories, even when we're not consciously aware of it. This is because the subconscious mind is constantly processing information, memories, and emotions, and it often weaves these elements together to form new narratives and concepts. It's the source of our dreams, sudden bursts of inspiration, and those 'aha' moments when ideas seemingly materialize out of nowhere."

He paused for a moment, allowing Deven to absorb his words. "While the subconscious can be a wellspring of innovation," he continued, "it's also where our fears, anxieties, and unresolved issues can manifest, sometimes in unexpected ways. Understanding and harnessing the power of the subconscious mind can lead to greater creativity, self-awareness, and personal growth. But also it has its adverse effects if negative thoughts have started rooting there"

Deven nodded in agreement, realizing that this explanation shed light on the mysterious experiences his family had encountered in Shanti Villa. It made him more determined than ever to uncover the truth behind those unsettling events.

Sadly, he eventually stopped coming to therapy, and after a few months, I saw his missing person's report in the newspaper. It was indeed a deeply saddening outcome for me, as I was unable to help him during his most challenging times."

Dr. Rathi's words had a profound impact on Deven. They confirmed his suspicions that the unsettling events in Shanti Villa were not mere psychological phenomena. It seemed highly improbable that two different individuals, Mr. Alok Joshi and Mrs. Asha Joshi, would independently experience such similar hallucinations. Deven now believed that there was indeed something far more ominous and sinister at play in that house, something beyond the realm of psychology.

His determination to uncover the truth was stronger than ever. He knew he had to delve deeper into this mystery and find a way to confront whatever malevolent force had plagued the lives of the Joshi family and others who had lived in Shanti Villa.

Deven was now on his way to meet the third and arguably the most crucial person in Mrs. Asha Joshi's life – Sadh guru Govind Ji. The way she had spoken about him, it was clear that he possessed some extraordinary divine energy. He had been her guide and protector for several years, providing her with a shield against the malevolent forces that seemed to haunt Shanti Villa.

As he approached the ashram, Deven couldn't help but marvel at its serenity. Mrs. Asha had described it as a haven on earth in her diary, and it was easy to see why. The place exuded an aura of tranquility and spirituality, nestled amidst the natural beauty of the surroundings. Deven hoped that here, in this spiritual haven, he would find the answers to the questions that had been haunting him ever since he stumbled upon the secrets of Shanti Villa.

As Deven entered Sadhguru Govind Ji's ashram, he was immediately struck by its unique blend of tradition and modernity. The ashram was like a school where the ancient Vedic shastras, Ayurveda, and astrology were taught alongside cutting-edge science and technology. There was a well-equipped science lab where students delved into experiments and discoveries, an astronomy observatory where they gazed at the cosmos, and a vast library housing an extensive collection of books on a wide range of subjects.

The ashram was a place where people from all walks of life came seeking peace and solace. It offered courses in yoga, Vipassana, and meditation, providing a serene environment for spiritual growth and self-discovery. Sadhguru Govind Ji himself met with people, addressing their queries in his unique and profound way, imparting wisdom and guidance that transcended the mundane.

The ashram had a rich history of hosting visits from many great and important individuals, not only from India but from various parts of the world. It had earned recognition and accolades in diverse fields. Students here had achieved international recognition, winning awards in astronomy, excelling in science exhibitions, and even making their mark in sports at the international level.

This ashram was unlike typical religious institutions that often exploited people in the name of faith. Instead, it was a harmonious blend of science, arts, spirituality, and culture, where knowledge was revered, and wisdom was sought. Deven couldn't help but be awed by the holistic and progressive approach of Sadhguru Govind Ji's ashram.

Deven's curiosity led him to a deep dive into the world of Sadhguru Govind Ji. As he googled the name, he found a treasure trove of articles, videos, and interviews where Govind Ji discussed a wide array of topics ranging from nature and the environment to astronomy, astrology, spirituality, and even the intricate realms of manifestation and Mantra-Tantra. It was evident that Govind Ji possessed a profound knowledge that spanned across both science and spirituality.

To Deven's surprise, he discovered that Govind Ji was a highly educated individual with a deep love for science. His experiments had garnered recognition on a global scale. He held more than ten degrees at a relatively young age, showcasing his exceptional academic prowess. Yet, Govind Ji had chosen a path where science and spirituality converged seamlessly.

But what truly amazed Deven was the multifaceted nature of Govind Ji's personality. In his 50s, he not only delved into the depths of spirituality but also enjoyed playing golf and practicing the guitar. This extraordinary individual had a fan base that spanned across various domains, including celebrities, sports players, and politicians. Despite his fame, Govind Ji remained accessible to all, a quality that resonated deeply with Deven. It was clear that he had become an ardent admirer of this remarkable person.

As Deven settled into the amphitheater, he eagerly awaited the arrival of Sadhguru Govind Ji. His anticipation grew as he had become an ardent admirer of this remarkable man's personality. When Govind Ji finally appeared, Deven was struck by his presence.

Despite being in his 50s, Govind Ji looked a decade younger, exuding vitality and health that suggested a regular exercise regimen. He wore a simple yet elegant attire, consisting of a khaki shirt and beige pants. But what truly stood out was the natural glow on his face, a testament to the inner peace and contentment he seemed to radiate.

As Govind Ji took his place on the floor, seated on a plain rug, he welcomed everyone with a warm smile. His aura exuded tranquility and wisdom. Today, the topic of his discourse was faith, and he began by sharing a mythological story about the devotion of Bhakt Prahlad. Deven was captivated by his words, drawn into the narrative that seamlessly wove spirituality and storytelling.

Sadhguru Govind Ji continued to narrate the captivating story of young Prahlad and the triumph of faith over evil. The audience was enraptured by his words as he described the unwavering devotion of Prahlad and the relentless attempts of King Hiranyakashipu to break that faith.

In a kingdom far away, Prahlad's father, King Hiranyakashipu, was a proud and arrogant ruler. He demanded that his son worship him instead of Lord Vishnu, but Prahlad's faith remained steadfast. He believed in the omnipresence of God, a belief that no force could shake.

The king grew increasingly infuriated with his son's devotion and attempted various tricks and trials to change Prahlad's beliefs. Each time, Lord Vishnu intervened to protect his unwavering devotee.

As the story unfolded, King Hiranyakashipu, in a fit of rage, challenged Prahlad to reveal the whereabouts of Lord Vishnu, even striking a massive pillar with his mace. To the astonishment of all present, the pillar cracked open, and Lord Vishnu emerged in the form of Narasimha, a half-man, half-lion deity. He defeated the evil king and took him on His lap.

Prahlad's faith had triumphed, and Lord Vishnu rewarded him for his steadfast devotion. Prahlad went on to become a wise and just king, known for his compassion and humility. His story served as a powerful reminder that even the smallest seed of faith can move mountains, and that in the end, goodness and faith always prevail over evil.

As Deven listened to Sadhguru Govind Ji's rendition of the timeless tale, it resonated with a deeper significance than he had ever felt before. While he had heard this story in his childhood, this time its message about the triumph of good over evil, the unwavering power of faith and devotion, and the ultimate victory of righteousness had a profound impact on him. It was as if a new light had illuminated his path, filling him with a newfound determination. Deven was now certain that Sadhguru Govind Ji would be his guiding force in this journey, his Sarthi, as he embarked on a quest for truth and discovery in the enigmatic world of Shanti Villa.

As the people around him began to ask questions and seek solutions from Sadhguru Govind Ji, Deven couldn't help but notice the simplicity and practicality of the remedies being offered. These weren't the typical superstitious or ritualistic approaches often associated with such discussions. Instead, Sadhguru's guidance revolved around making small but meaningful changes in daily routines and lifestyles.

The solutions were refreshingly straightforward: altering travel routes, changing eating habits, repositioning household objects to channel energy more positively. It was about redirecting and harmonizing the energy in one's life, removing obstacles in the form of negative influences through the simplest and most practical means.

Deven patiently waited his turn, hoping for a more private discussion where he could delve deeper into these unconventional but enlightening insights.

Deven watched as the gathering gradually dispersed, and when only he and Sadh guru Govind Ji remained, he mustered the courage to approach the spiritual guru. Govind Ji, still seated in a meditative posture, opened his eyes slowly and regarded Deven with a penetrating gaze. It was as if he was assessing Deven's intentions and sincerity. After a moment, he gracefully rose to his feet, breaking into a warm smile as he addressed Deven.

"Alright, young man," Govind Ji began, "I sense you have questions. Let's continue our conversation while we take a stroll, shall we? How about some green tea? It's nearly 7, and I'm quite particular about my diet," he added with a playful grin. Deven was pleasantly surprised by Govind Ji's friendly and approachable demeanor. In that moment, the age difference seemed to dissolve, and while the utmost respect was ever-present, Govind Ji had a way of making Deven feel like he was catching up with an old friend.

As they walked, Sadhguru Govind Ji engaged Deven in a casual conversation, asking about his life, job, and family. Deven shared his story briefly, recounting the loss of his parents during childhood, his years in a hostel, and his academic achievements that had led to his current senior position at a renowned MNC.

Govind Ji paused in their walk, turned to Deven, and placed a friendly arm around his shoulder. He spoke with admiration, "You're one tough, self-made man, indeed."

Their conversation eventually led them to a cafeteria near the amphitheater. Govind Ji entered the space, and Deven followed suit. There, Govind Ji politely offered Deven some green tea. Deven, feeling somewhat overwhelmed by the guru's kindness, accepted the offer.

To Deven's surprise, Govind Ji personally prepared the tea. Deven hesitated and said, "Sadhguru, I thought you would call an assistant or someone to make the tea. Now, I feel awkward."

Govind Ji smiled warmly and replied, "Here in this place, we teach everyone to be self-sufficient. Why should I be privileged? Doing my own work is something I have always practiced. It has made me very independent."

Deven couldn't help but admire Govind Ji's humility and simplicity.

After taking a sip of the green tea, Govind Ji turned his attention toward Deven and began the conversation. He inquired, "So, Deven, what brings you here today? I sense you carry a burden of doubts and questions. Tell me, what's on your mind?"

Deven expressed his gratitude with a sincere tone, saying, "Firstly, Sadhguru, I want to express my deep appreciation for your willingness to sit here with me and listen to my questions. Thank you; it means a lot."

Deven went on to explain his situation, revealing, "I recently inherited this property," as he displayed a photo of the house on his cell phone. "The previous owner, Mrs. Asha Joshi, visited you a couple of years ago after her husband's mysterious disappearance from their house." Deven handed over her diary, open to the page where her meeting with Govind Ji was highlighted. He also showed Govind Ji a photo of Asha Ji.

Continuing his narrative, Deven recounted, "At that time, you mentioned that some answers are not simple. Whatever energy that house contained, it was undoubtedly formidable and challenging. You advised her to conduct a small experiment to gain insight into what she was up against and what answers she sought. She certainly witnessed something malevolent, and she couldn't muster the courage to seek your guidance to continue the battle. She ended up losing the fight without even beginning. However, the simple path you showed her, where you encouraged her to perform regular prayers, somehow protected her. But eventually, she gave up."

Deven paused and looked into Govind Ji's eyes with sincerity, saying, "I have a humble request. I need to find out exactly what was there in that house. I can sense something very sinister and malevolent. Is there any way I can provide closure and justice to the Joshi family? The way you had warned her indicates you had sensed something negative. If you can enlighten me a little about that please?

Govind Ji carefully reviewed the diary and the highlighted sections Deven had pointed out. After a profound sigh and about 20 minutes of contemplation, he leaned back in his chair and looked at Deven with a thoughtful expression.

Then, breaking the silence, Govind Ji suggested, "Do you have the keys to your house now, Deven? Let's go and see the place personally."

Deven was taken aback and momentarily stunned by the sudden proposal. "You, Sadhguru, are coming to Shanti Villa?" he exclaimed, a mixture of shock and gratitude in his voice. "I thought you were here to guide us, not physically accompany us. I can't express how thankful I am."

Govind Ji, with a playful glint in his eye, replied, "Deven, I'm here to offer guidance, and my path is to illuminate the way for those who possess the courage and willingness to do something good and positive. Don't worry; it's still your battle. You see, In the epic Mahabharata, Lord Krishna served as the charioteer (sarthi) for Arjuna, guiding him through the battlefield of Kurukshetra. Despite possessing the formidable Sudarshan Chakra capable of ending the war instantly, Krishna chose not to take up arms. His presence alone, as the voice of wisdom and moral guidance, added immeasurable value to the conflict. Krishna's decision was a profound lesson for future generations, demonstrating that true power lies not in the mere use of force but in righteousness, wisdom, and selfless guidance. His role as a divine charioteer symbolized the importance of making morally sound choices and upholding dharma, even in the face of adversity. I sense your sincerity, and that's why I'm here. So, why waste time?"

Govind Ji left to retrieve his keys and prepare for the visit. Deven watched in amazement as Govind Ji returned about 15 minutes later, dressed in comfortable track suits and sport shoes. With car keys in hand, Govind Ji invited, "Let's go."

Deven was still absorbing the transformation he was witnessing in Govind Ji, who simply smiled and said, "Don't be surprised, my friend. After this, I need to fit in my jog," he added with a chuckle.

With that, Govind Ji opened the door to his luxurious Range Rover, settled into the driver's seat, and started the car. They were on their way to Shanti Villa, embarking on a journey that held the promise of answers and the potential to confront the malevolent forces lurking within the old mansion.

As they reached the gate, Deven hurried to open the door for Govind Ji. However, before he could reach, Govind Ji leaped from his car, exuding youthful energy as he warmed up by hopping and jumping. "Deven," he said with a warm smile, "give me the keys. I'll take a quick look around the house, inside too. You can sit in the car while I explore." This selfless gesture from Govind Ji added yet another layer of surprise to Deven's day, leaving him truly touched by his friend's generosity.

As Govind Ji went inside Shanti Villa, Deven watched in anticipation. After a few moments, he noticed the lights flicker to life from within the house. First, the ground floor, then the upper floor, and finally, even the attic illuminated. Intriguingly, after about 20 minutes, the lights extinguished in the same order. Govind Ji emerged from the house, his countenance still revealing little. He resumed his place in the car, and Deven patiently waited for him to break the silence.

Eventually, Govind Ji turned to Deven and asked, "Deven, where do you live? Let me drop you at your place."

Deven replied, "I stay in Baner, Govind Ji. It shouldn't be too far from the Ashram."

Govind Ji smiled gently and said, "Don't worry about the distance. We need to have a little chat, and it's also time for me to experience your hospitality. I hope you don't mind me coming over."

This was yet another surprise from the unassuming man. As they drove, they discussed sports, the countries Govind Ji had traveled to, and his adventurous experiences. Deven found himself thoroughly enjoying Govind Ji's company. For a while, he forgot that this man had just come from a place where eerie happenings occurred. Govind Ji's calm demeanor, Deven thought, might be an effort to put him at ease.

As they arrived near Deven's apartment, Govind Ji parked his car. Deven was utterly mesmerized, finding it hard to believe that Govind Ji had invited himself over. He unlocked the apartment door, and they both entered. Deven guided him to the couch and excused himself to prepare some snacks and coffee.

Govind Ji, looking around the well-maintained apartment, remarked, "Deven, you've kept your house so nicely. It seems you're used to taking care of yourself, always, right?"

Deven smiled and replied, "Well, I never really had any other option, and besides, in the hostel, they teach you to do everything on your own."

Govind Ji smiled warmly and said, "You know, Deven, we teach the exact same thing in our ashram and gurukul. So, why were you surprised when I drove my car and made you green tea?"

Deven chuckled, realizing that their teachings indeed aligned and that his surprise had been unwarranted.

In the dimly lit living room of Deven's apartment, the weight of unspoken questions hung heavily in the air. Govind Ji, his eyes reflecting a blend of curiosity and concern, finally broke the silence.

"Okay, Deven," he began, his voice carrying the gravity of the moment. "Let's address the elephant in the room now. You must be curious to know why I asked for a visit to Shanti Villa and what I experienced. But, Deven, I need to know a few things too."

He leaned forward, his gaze locking onto Deven's, as if searching for answers within his very soul. "Why are you not selling that property? It's the easiest way to rid yourself of its burdens, not to mention the significant wealth it could bring you. Any man in your place would jump at such an opportunity. Why do you feel compelled to dig so deep, to put yourself at risk? I'm certain you've experienced something, and yet you continue to pursue a battle that isn't inherently yours. Is this about self-discovery, alongside unraveling truths hidden within those walls for longer than memory serves?"

Deven took a pause, his thoughts diving into the depths of his own motivations. It was a moment of profound introspection, one he had not dared to venture into before. His decision to retain the property was driven by instincts, but it was far from impulsive; it was a journey into uncharted territories, one that seemed destined to reveal the enigmatic secrets lurking within Shanti Villa's shadows.

Deven's voice trembled as he spoke, his emotions laid bare before Govind Ji. "Sadhguru," he began, "I've never truly had someone of my own, never felt that profound connection with anyone. When my parents tragically died in that fateful car accident, I was a mere 3 years old. I never had the chance to know them that well and my memories are almost not their with them to feel any connection to them, I never experienced the pain of loss of someone I truly felt connected to. It was just me, alone, as I grew up."

He paused, his gaze distant, as if recalling the lonely years of his youth. "And then," he continued, his voice softening, "one day, because of this lady, Mrs. Asha Joshi, my life transformed completely. Someone had never done anything like this for me before. Suddenly, I'm a millionaire, and I owe it all to her."

Deven's eyes welled up with gratitude and sorrow as he spoke of the woman who had changed the course of his life. "Even if I were to sell this house, Sadhguru," he whispered, his voice breaking, "if someone were to move in, their fate might mirror that of the Joshi family. I can't bear the thought of taking that sin upon my conscience. It's as if an unspoken responsibility rests on my shoulders, a duty to honor the memory of the

Joshi family."

Deven, with a mixture of anticipation and apprehension, awaited Guruji's response. After Deven had poured his heart out, Govind Ji's eyes held a deep sense of admiration and understanding.

"Deven," sadh guru replied with a profound sincerity, "I truly appreciate your courage and this selfless act. There are not many people on this earth who possess the depth of empathy and responsibility that you do."

sadhguru's gaze bore into Deven's soul as he continued, "I'm not here to influence your decision, my friend. It's your choice, entirely yours to make. But I must warn you, this path you've chosen is not an easy one. Whatever you're about to face will challenge you in ways you've never imagined, testing you on every parameter of your being. There will be moments when you might question why you embarked on this unconventional journey. However, your unwavering belief in yourself and your indomitable courage will be your guiding lights through this formidable ordeal."

With a deep breath, Sadh guru posed the pivotal question, "So, Deven, are you ready?" It was a question that transcended the boundaries of ordinary existence, one that called upon Deven to make a profound choice, one that would shape the course of his destiny.

Deven's gaze remained locked with Govind Ji's, a steely determination burning within his eyes. With unwavering resolve, he replied, "I don't have any other choice." His words echoed with a resolute commitment to the path he had chosen, a path laden with mystery, responsibility, and the weight of unforeseen challenges.

Sadhguru's countenance lit up with a radiant glow, his eyes sparkling with admiration as he beheld Deven's unwavering courage. A mischievous and playful smile danced upon his lips throughout their conversation, as though he had been testing Deven, pushing him to the edge of his resolve. It was a moment of profound connection between guru and disciple, where unspoken understanding passed between them, forging a bond that would carry them through the enigmatic journey that lay ahead.

"Okay, Deven," Govind Ji began, his voice carrying a sense of gravity, "so, are we ready to follow the exact same path I asked Asha Joshi to tread?"

Deven nodded, his resolve unwavering. "Yes, Govind Ji. I believe in God, although not in the conventional way. I have faith; I know He watches over me, but I've never adhered to the routine of performing religious rituals myself. I do visit Radha Krishna temple every Monday, though it's right here in our building."

Govind Ji smiled warmly. "That's perfectly fine, Deven. Faith, mixed with courage and self-belief, will play a major role here. Your devotion will be symbolic. Every morning and evening, you need to visit Shanti Villa, taking a small Krishna idol or a photo with you. Light a diya and dhoop there, offer prasad to God, and then place the prasad and diya near the door that leads upstairs. There's no need to ascend; that door is nearly invisible to those who reside above. Do this and return. Let's see what transpires after two days."

Govind Ji's eyes held a reassuring conviction. "Also, if you have the house plan, I'd like to see it. I'll return it when we meet the day after tomorrow. Now, rest up. I'll take my leave." He leaned in, his eyes filled with pride. "And yes, Deven, I am proud of you, dear."

Deven felt a mixture of emotions coursing through him - trepidation, faith, and an undeniable sense of purpose. This was the beginning of a journey that would test his beliefs, courage, and inner strength in ways he had never imagined.

After Govind Ji left, Deven retired to his bed, the weight of the day's revelations and decisions pressing upon him. As he lay there, lost in the dimly lit solitude of his bedroom, he couldn't help but reflect on the abrupt twist that had transformed his once mundane corporate life. He had shifted from the predictable routine of a corporate job to embarking on a journey against something and someone that belonged to the sinister realms of the world.

However, amidst the uncertainty and the shadows that loomed ahead, Govind Ji's unwavering support and guidance were like a beacon of light. They illuminated the path that Deven had chosen to tread, casting aside the cloak of mundanity and leading him toward a destiny filled with enigmas and challenges he could scarcely imagine. It was a journey that would test his beliefs, courage, and resilience, but it was also a journey that held the promise of self-discovery and the unveiling of truths that had long been concealed in the darkness.

CHAPTER SEVEN

The Chase Begins

That night, as Deven drifted into the realm of dreams, it was no surprise that his recent experiences would infiltrate his slumber. In his dream, he found himself standing before the nursery door at Shanti Villa, bathed in the soft, ethereal glow of the moonlight seeping through the window. As he watched in astonishment, the door slowly creaked open, revealing four figures, luminous and cloud-like, meandering about the room and hovering over a table. Gradually, they formed a circle, rotating around the table, and then they stopped. One of these apparitions, bearing an uncanny resemblance to Asha Ji, fixed her gaze upon Deven. She gestured, causing the other three figures to turn their attention to him as well.

Deven's heart raced, his instincts urging him to flee from this otherworldly encounter. But, paradoxically, as fear coursed through his veins, he planted his feet firmly before the door. His heart pounded, and he could feel the pressure of his own prayers welling up within him. With trembling hands held together in prayer, he closed his eyes, beseeching divine protection. Yet, he did not retreat or flee; he remained resolute.

Suddenly, a brilliant flash of light enveloped him, and there, in the midst of this radiant effulgence, Deven saw a Morpankh, a divine symbol that filled him with an inexplicable serenity. And just as swiftly as the light had enveloped him, he was transported back to his apartment, where the warm embrace of the morning sun bathed his face.

Deven awoke, his mind a tumultuous whirlwind of emotions and questions. What had he witnessed? Those eerie figures, and then the Morpankh that had come to his rescue—did it symbolize Govind Ji's presence in his life and on his impending journey? Confused but undeterred, Deven arose from his slumber and gazed out from his balcony. The sun, a symbol of new beginnings, cast its glow upon him. With folded hands, Deven paid homage to the sun, a ritual he would carry into his morning, signaling the dawn of yet another day, a day that would lead him back to Shanti Villa, ready to embark on a journey filled with faith, courage, and the promise of discovery. With resolute steps, he went about his morning routine, preparing for the journey that lay ahead.

One item he held close to his heart was a small idol of Lord Krishna it had a beautiful morpankh on the crown of lord Krishna . It had belonged to his mother and had been a cherished part of his life for as long as he could remember. Today, it would accompany him to Shanti Villa as a symbol of faith and protection.

Deven also gathered two cans of water, intending to clean the sacred space before performing his rituals. He was adamant about not using anything from Shanti Villa, not even a drop of its water. He packed some paper plates, Haldi (turmeric), Kumkum (vermilion), and a selection of colourful flowers for his pooja.

With all his preparations complete, Deven booked an Uber, and it soon arrived to take him to Shanti Villa. As he stepped into the car, he carried with him not only these tangible items but also a renewed sense of purpose and a heart filled with unwavering resolve. Today marked the beginning of a journey that held the promise of unraveling mysteries and discovering truths hidden within the enigmatic walls of Shanti Villa.

It was 9 o'clock in the morning when Deven pushed open the door to Shanti Villa. In the bright daylight, the house seemed transformed, its grandeur masking the eerie secrets that lurked within its walls. With a sense of determination, Deven moved through the house, his purpose clear.

Before beginning his pooja, he stopped by the sink to wash his hands with the water he bought from his apartment, wanting to start with a sense of purity. Then, he made his way to the mandir room, a place that held a unique significance in the house. With the cans of water, he had brought, he carefully cleaned the room, washing away any traces of the past.

Next, he placed the small idol of Lord Krishna on the platform, an item that had been a part of his life since his childhood. Deven lit a diya, allowing its flickering flame to cast a warm, golden light in the room. The sweet scent of dhoop filled the air as he burned it in offering. With reverence, he presented prasad and a vibrant assortment of flowers to the idol, seeking blessings and protection.

Holding haldi and kumkum in a paper plate he had brought from home, he marked the idol, signifying its sanctity. With deep devotion, he chanted a small shlok, the sacred words resonating in the room: "ॐ नमो भगवते वासुदेवाय" (Om Namo Bhagavate Vasudevaya).

His rituals complete, Deven took another diya and the paper plate holding prasad and flowers, carefully placing them near the door that led to the upper floor. With a sense of solemnity, he locked the main door behind him and exited Shanti Villa.

Until now, every visit to the villa had been in the safety of daylight, but Govind Ji's instructions now demanded that Deven perform his evening pooja as well. The prospect of facing the house's mysteries in the shroud of darkness weighed heavily on his mind. Shanti Villa held a history of unsettling occurrences, most of which unfolded in the obscurity of the night, and this next part of his journey was undoubtedly the most challenging.

As he came back to his apartment, Deven's mind remained preoccupied with the task that lay ahead - the evening pooja at Shanti Villa. He watched some web series on Netflix to pass the time, but his thoughts constantly circled back to the daunting prospect of returning to the villa in the dark.

Ordering food online, he made an attempt to eat, but his nerves got the best of him, and he hardly touched his meal. The hours passed slowly, and as the evening descended, around 6:30, he knew it was time to embark on the next part of his journey.

Once again, he called an Uber, determined to complete the evening pooja with the same devotion as he had in the morning. Fresh flowers and prasad were tucked beside him, and he carried the water bottles, ready to follow the same rituals that he had performed earlier in the day. The night held secrets, and as he stepped into the car, a sense of trepidation mixed with resolve filled his heart. Shanti Villa awaited him, its mysteries and challenges concealed within the veil of darkness.

The villa stood in eerie stillness within the shroud of darkness. The gnarled trees surrounding the house seemed to partake in a sinister shadow dance, their twisted branches casting ominous figures on the house's facade. Deven had pledged to himself not to utilize anything within the house, including its electricity, as he remained steadfast in his resolve.

With a trembling hand, he illuminated a torch from his mobile phone, its feeble light cutting through the pitch-black night. Slowly, he swung open the main gate, the creaking noise echoing in the silence, amplifying the pounding of his own heart, which resounded in his ears like a malevolent drumbeat.

Guided by the feeble glow of his phone's torch, he retraced his steps to the mandir. With great trepidation, he lit the diya, offered prasad and flowers, and burned the dhoop as he had earlier that morning.

Yet, the most challenging part remained: checking the door connecting to the upper floor, where he needed to place the diya and prasad plate. As he reached that ominous door, he saw it—a haunting tableau that struck terror into his very soul. The offerings he had placed there earlier—burnt flowers and desiccated fruits—lay in the exact arrangement Asha Ji had described during her ritual. Deven knew this was coming, yet the sight sent shivers down his spine. He cleaned the remnants and replaced them with a freshly lit diya, prasad plate, and flowers.

As he began to turn away, an unsettling hiss reverberated through the air, causing his feet to freeze in their tracks. He turned to locate the source of the sound and witnessed a sight beyond belief. A golden light emanated from the mandir's diya he had just lit, while its counterpart, an eerie replica of the house, displayed a red-hued glow from the identical diya in Asha Ji's room.

The hiss persisted, now accompanied by an unsettling cacophony of demonic sounds. Inexplicably, the replica mirrored Deven's own actions, but this time, there was no idol in the mandir. Slowly, the figure turned toward him, revealing a reflection of himself in that sinister parallel world. A malevolent grin spread across the face in the other realm, and the intensity of the red light grew.

An inexplicable urgency overcame Deven, and he backed away hastily. The hissing and demonic sounds multiplied, and the red light intensified. Deven rushed out of the house, slamming the door shut and locking it behind him. His body was drenched in sweat despite the wintry chill in the air. He knew he had to share this horrifying experience with Sadh guru, so he swiftly booked a cab to the ashram.

As he settled into the car's seat, he began to breathe once more, realizing that he had been holding his breath throughout this terrifying encounter with the supernatural forces that lurked within Shanti Villa.

As Deven arrived at the ashram, he found that Govind Ji had just concluded his Satsang session. Restlessness gnawed at him, an urgent need to share his harrowing experience with the supernatural forces dwelling within Shanti Villa. He needed answers about the parallel dimension, the sinister mimicry of his pooja, the ominous warning that surrounded the villa, and the malevolent imitation of his own actions.

Unable to sit still, Deven's anxiety was palpable. However, Govind Ji, noticing his distressed state, calmly raised his hand in a reassuring gesture, signaling Deven to wait. His expression conveyed that there would be a time and place for Deven to reveal the chilling ordeal he had just faced. For now, patience and stillness were required.

After some time, Govind Ji beckoned Deven to follow him. Govind Ji moved with such swiftness that Deven had to nearly jog to keep pace. They arrived at Govind Ji's meditation room, a serene and sacred space filled with an aura of tranquility. Lush green plants adorned the room, their leaves glistening with health. A small water fountain burbled gently in one corner, its soothing sound contributing to the room's peaceful ambiance. Soft instrumental music played in the background, further enhancing the sense of calm.

Govind Ji settled onto his meditation asana with grace, and he gestured for Deven to sit on an asana placed in front of him. Deven, his anxiety mounting, began to speak, but Govind Ji raised his hand, a signal for silence. He instructed Deven to sit and follow his lead.

Deven's anxiety continued to mount as he awaited Govind Ji's guidance and the opportunity to share the unsettling experiences that had shaken his resolve and tested his faith.

Govind Ji gracefully settled into a meditation pose, his hands forming a sacred mudra as he began to chant "Om." His eyes remained closed in deep concentration.

With a calm and assured demeanor, he gestured for Deven to follow suit.

Deven joined in, albeit with a hint of anxiety and a touch of irritation. He couldn't comprehend why Govind Ji was seemingly engrossed in this meditation, seemingly ignoring the pressing matter he was eager to share. Yet, he complied, mimicking the mudra and participating in the chant, albeit with a restless mind that longed to unburden itself of the ominous experiences he had endured.

As Deven continued to follow the meditative practice instructed by Govind Ji, he gradually felt himself sinking into a deep state of meditation. It was as if he was being drawn into a profound slumber of the mind. In this meditative state, he once again encountered the brilliant light, followed by the vibrant Morpankh. He sensed the Morpankh's ethereal presence moving over his head, then descending gently over his shoulders and throughout his body.

A remarkable sense of tranquility washed over him, and his internal systems seemed to harmonize with this soothing presence. The melodious strains of instrumental music, featuring the sweet tune of a flute, caressed his senses. In the midst of this serene experience, Deven suddenly became aware of a warm hand resting on his shoulder.

He opened his eyes, and there, before him, was Govind Ji, his face adorned with a serene and knowing smile. It was as if Govind Ji had guided him through this meditative journey, and Deven had experienced a profound connection with the divine during his brief encounter with the Morpankh.

"Deven, I hope you're feeling better now," said Govind Ji, his mischievous smile once again gracing his face. Before Deven could utter a word, Govind Ji continued, his tone grave and wise, "Deven, you must understand that what you're confronting is undeniably formidable. You've undoubtedly encountered something harrowing. However, remember this: fear is their sustenance. Today, through your small act of spirituality, you've ignited a disturbance in their realm. It's akin to disturbing a beehive, and now the bees are not only furious but also deeply unsettled. You've ventured into their territory by an act that has compelled them to pause and reevaluate."

Govind Ji's words carried both caution and wisdom. Deven had indeed embarked on a treacherous path, one that would demand unwavering courage and resilience as he delved deeper into the mysteries and malevolent forces that inhabited Shanti Villa.

"I just want to know; do you want to continue it?" Govind Ji asked Deven, looking deep into his eyes. Deven's mind flashed with memories of everything he had experienced thus far. He paused, taking in Govind Ji's question, and then inquired, "So, this means I have to continue performing the pooja at Shanti Villa, right?"

Govind Ji maintained unwavering eye contact with Deven and replied with a gentle smile, "Yes, dear. And I have something for you." He disappeared briefly into a small room adjacent to the meditation space, returning with a small Morpankh. It was fashioned like a brooch, and Govind Ji secured it to Deven's sweater with a clip. "This looks great on you," he remarked warmly. "Deven, you are an exceptionally brave and selfless individual. Your strength lies in your goodness, and it will fortify you in the battle ahead. This isn't merely a confrontation with the malevolent forces within Shanti Villa; it's a battle against your own weaknesses—doubt, fear. Your weapons are your courage and your unwavering faith. Trust yourself, and leave the rest to God. Remember, He stands beside you."

With these words of wisdom, Govind Ji patted Deven's back and placed a hand on his head. Deven instinctively bent down to touch Govind Ji's feet, seeking his blessings for the impending struggle. As he rode in the Uber back to his apartment, he reflected on his day, from the unsettling dream to the encounter with the sinister presence within Shanti Villa. A Morpankh had come to his aid when he had stood steadfast, an act that had held a profound message. Govind Ji had imparted invaluable advice—God assists those who first help themselves, especially those who possess the courage and kindness to do so. Deven looked at the Morpankh brooch with a smile, embracing the newfound purpose and strength it symbolized.

Pawns and Predators

Another day dawned, and Deven had enjoyed a remarkably peaceful night's sleep. The Morpankh brooch, a token of his newfound resolve, still adorned his sweater. As he awakened, his fingers naturally gravitated towards it. Following his morning routine, he stepped onto his balcony to greet the day with a respectful Namaste.

After a refreshing shower, he embarked on his daily pilgrimage to Shanti Villa. The routine was familiar now – lighting the diya, offering prayers, and carefully placing prasad and flowers near the door to the upper floor. But today, something was different. The malevolent forces within Shanti Villa seemed agitated, displaying their fury through their actions. The remnants of yesterday's pooja lay in tatters, torn paper plates and burnt offerings telling a tale of anger and resentment.

Deven remained unfazed. He calmly cleaned the mess, replacing it with fresh offerings, flowers, and a lit diya. As he exited Shanti Villa, he couldn't ignore the growing sense of foreboding. Today's display of malevolence was a clear indication that he had disregarded the ominous warning given by the demonic entity residing there.

Determined to keep his mind occupied, Deven decided to spend the day watching a movie and indulging in some retail therapy at the nearby mall. He knew the intensity of the challenges ahead was mounting, but he consciously avoided dwelling on the fear that threatened to consume him. Instead, he sought solace in the Morpankh brooch, a constant reminder of his commitment and the courage required to face the looming darkness.

Somehow, Deven managed to pass the time until evening, all the while feeling the weight of impending dread. As the sun began its descent, he steeled himself for another visit to Shanti Villa, fully aware that the malevolent entity within would likely be more furious today. Gathering his resolve, he purchased fresh flowers and a box of sweets to offer as prasad, and his trembling hand clutched a water bottle for courage. The path ahead was treacherous, but Deven knew he had to confront this darkness head-on.

As he entered, Deven lit the torchlight from his phone, its feeble glow cutting through the darkness of Shanti Villa. He made his way with trembling steps to the mandir room, a place now haunted by sinister memories. Cleaning the room, he couldn't help but steal a glance behind him, where he had witnessed the malevolent imitation of his own pooja, a grotesque parody of his devotion.

But Deven forced his mind back to the task at hand, recollecting Govind ji's guidance. He needed faith in himself and in a higher power. With meticulous care, he cleaned the mandir and tenderly tended to Lord Krishna's idol. Lighting two diyas, igniting dhoop, and adorning the idol with a fresh garland of jasmine flowers, the room was filled with a fragrant, serene aura.

Then came the time for his mantra, "ॐ नमो भगवते वासुदेवाय" (Om Namo Bhagavate Vasudevaya). As Deven chanted, he centered his chakras and focused solely on his breath, drawing strength and conviction from within. With folded hands, he implored God for courage and support, a silent plea echoing in the sanctum.

With renewed determination, he opened his eyes, ready for the most challenging part of his ritual: placing the diya on the upper floor's connecting door. His mind raced with memories of the previous day's desecration. Nevertheless, resolute and chanting his mantra, he began the journey toward that ominous door, each step infused with unwavering faith.

As Deven advanced toward the mandir, the atmosphere grew increasingly ominous. The gentle chanting of his mantra, "ॐ नमो, भगवते वासुदेवाय" (Om Namo Bhagavate Vasudevaya), was punctuated by a sudden, bone-chilling scream from the upper floor. For a brief moment, he froze in terror, but then, with sheer determination, he continued his sacred chant. The wails and screams intensified, echoing through Shanti Villa. Unearthly, dragging noises followed, and the house itself seemed to come alive, with doors, windows, rooms, and cupboards springing open with deafening thuds.

Deven knew he had triggered their fury, and there was no turning back. His heart raced as he kept up his mantra, beads of sweat forming on his forehead. Was retreat an option? The promise he made to himself, to Asha Devi, and the faith Govind Ji had placed in him all flashed through his mind. No, retreating was not an option. He had to stand his ground.

With trembling hands, he approached the door to the upper floor. As he gingerly placed the diya and plate with flowers and prasad on the threshold, the world around him seemed to collapse into an sudden eerie silence, broken only by his own racing heartbeat. He felt trapped and wondered if this was the end. Had he embarked on this journey only to meet a sinister fate?

His mind spiraled into doubt and fear, but then he remembered Govind Ji's words. He had to trust himself and leave the rest to God. With newfound resolve, he turned his gaze back to the mandir, intending to seek solace in his faith. The silence was deafening. Deven was acutely aware of the heavy metal lock securing the upper floor's connecting door. Yet, as he watched in disbelief, it disintegrated into pieces before his eyes,

And the door swung open....

Deven's heart pounded, his breaths came in ragged gasps. Beyond the door, he saw figures emerging—a ghastly, disfigured assembly of Asha Devi, Alok, Shanti Devi, and Anand Ji. These were the very people who had vanished from this house, now standing before him in a demonic state. Deven was paralyzed by terror, trapped in a world where the air grew scorching hot, and a putrid stench pervaded the atmosphere, choking him.

He clutched his Krishna idol and his Morpankh broach to his chest ,and closed his eyes, reciting his mantra. The air grew hotter, and the malevolent figures drew closer, circling him with wicked smiles, their red eyes fixed on him. Deven's thoughts raced. Had he failed? Was this the end?

But then he remembered Govind Ji's teachings—belief in oneself, faith in a higher power. With resolve bordering on anger, Deven shifted into dhyana mudra, his chakras aligning. As the eerie figures continued their macabre dance, he felt himself slowly lifted into the air. Panic clawed at him, but he did not open his eyes.

Suddenly, he was transported back in time. He was a child, sitting in the back seat of a car, his parents in the front. It was Janmashtami, and he was dressed as Krishna. Laughter and familial banter filled the air. But then, a horrifying accident unfolded. A truck collided with their car, sending it plummeting from a flyover. Deven witnessed the agony in his parents' eyes, their faces contorted in pain. Darkness overcame him, and he lost consciousness.

A Morpankh part of his outfit that day was clutched tightly to his chest, it was the only memory that deven had after the crash. Days later, he woke up in a hospital, miraculously unharmed. His parents, however, were gone forever.

As his consciousness returned to the present, Deven found himself suspended in mid-air, the entities encircling him. Yet something had changed. His fear had transformed into anger, an anger fueled by years of grief and loss. His closed eyes glowed with an inner light, and he clung to his Krishna idol with unshakable determination.

The morpankh brooch, given to him by Govind ji, suddenly emitted a blinding light, illuminating the room with divine radiance. The eerie entities recoiled, their malevolence faltering in the face of this brilliant illumination. Deven felt a surge of energy coursing through him, as if he had become a conduit for a higher power.

The circle of figures began to shrink, their malevolence waning. The air cooled, and the pungent odor dissipated. Slowly, Deven descended to the ground. The entities had been defeated. As he lay on the ground, gasping for breath, the weight of his anger and newfound strength bore witness to his triumph over the malevolent forces that had plagued Shanti Villa.

Deven lay on the cold floor, utterly drained of energy. The ordeal had taken its toll on him, leaving him feeling exhausted and vulnerable. As he felt a gentle hand on his shoulder, he slowly opened his eyes and there he saw the glowing face of Govind ji. Relief washed over him. He knew Govind ji came for his rescue

Govind ji spoke reassuringly, "Deven, are you alright? Wake up." Deven managed to sit up, and Govind ji offered him a glass of water. Deven sipped it gratefully, the cool liquid soothing his parched throat.

"Come, beta," Govind ji said, guiding Deven to a chair. "Sit here, calm down. There's no need to speak just yet."

Deven took a deep breath, his trembling gradually subsiding. Govind ji switched on the lights, and the room was bathed in illumination. Deven looked at him with profound gratitude.

"Thank you, Govind ji," he said, his voice filled with sincerity. "Thanks for coming on time and saving me. I don't know what would have happened to me otherwise."

Govind ji regarded him with his mischievous smile and replied, "Deven, dear, I have done nothing. It was all you. I was just here to support you because in moments like this, people often lose their faith. But you, you did not lose your faith. And from that unwavering belief, a divine power emerged."

Govind ji's eyes gleamed with admiration as he continued, "I was here, Deven, in case something terrible happened and you needed help. But to my surprise, you did it all on your own. You heard your inner voice, tapped into your inner strength, and brought forth an energy that scared those evil entities away."

Deven listened intently, feeling a surge of pride mixed with the lingering adrenaline from the encounter. It was a strange feeling, knowing that he had confronted and repelled such malevolent forces.

"But," Govind ji's expression grew serious, "remember, Deven, those entities may have lost one battle, but it's not over yet. We need to finish this before their power gets refilled. The key lies in their epicenter, the nursery room. It's their central hub, their recharge station, and their hideout."

Deven nodded, absorbing Govind ji's words. The gravity of the situation weighed on him, but he also felt a newfound determination. He was no longer alone in this battle, and he had just discovered a source of strength within himself that he had never known existed. The next steps were clear – they had to confront the evil at its core and put an end to it once and for all. Deven leaned forward, hanging on to every word that Govind ji spoke. His heart pounded with a mixture of fear and anticipation. He was about to embark on a mission that was unlike anything he had ever imagined.

"And Deven," Govind ji continued, his voice carrying a sense of urgency, "this time, we are going on the offensive. No more playing defense. We have to enter their territory, confront what has lurked here for ages, and has consumed the souls of those who lived in this place. But you must understand, this won't be easy. Once they realize that you're here to destroy them, they'll unleash all their forces against you. They might play tricks on your mind, show you things that no common man should ever witness."

Deven shivered at the thought but steeled himself. He was prepared to face whatever horrors awaited him. Govind ji's guidance and his newfound inner strength were his pillars of support.

Govind ji's eyes held a mysterious glint as he added, "So, gather your strength, Deven. I want to show you something.

Govind ji reached into his pockets, his movements deliberate and purposeful. He retrieved a folded piece of paper, the house plan of Shanti Villa. Deven vividly remembered Govind ji taking this architectural drawing from him after their first visit to the villa. As Govind ji unfolded the paper and laid it on the dining table, it nearly covered the entire surface, emphasizing the gravity of what he was about to reveal.

With a measured gesture, Govind ji pointed to certain areas on the paper, his fingers tracing the dimensions outlined there. His eyes fixed on Deven, he began to explain, "Deven, here is the plan of the ground floor. According to this layout, the dimensions of this part, which is Asha ji and Alok ji's bedroom, are mentioned as 16*24. Now, if we look here," he continued, pointing to the paper, "the upper floor's nursery room is directly above Asha ji and Alok ji's bedroom. Logically, it should have the same dimensions, 16*24, as indicated in the plan. But during our visit to Shanti Villa, I noticed something was amiss with this nursery room."

As he spoke, Govind ji's finger moved to the area representing the nursery room. "Upon closer inspection, I measured the room myself and discovered that it's significantly smaller than what the plan suggests. This means that something exists behind the walls of the nursery room, something that was added later, something hidden from plain sight. Our answers, Deven, they lie behind those walls in the room above."

Deven's gaze followed Govind ji's movements as he spoke. He hung onto every word with a sense of profound determination. Today, he understood, was a pivotal moment, a do-or-die situation where he had to confront the unknown lurking within Shanti Villa.

As Govind ji gently took the Krishna idol and his broach from Deven's hands and placed it on a nearby table, Deven couldn't help but feel a bit perplexed. He had grown accustomed to carrying the idol with him, finding solace and courage in its presence. He hesitated before asking, "Govind ji, am I not supposed to take this idol with me?"

Govind ji responded with a reassuring smile, "You won't need that, my child. Now, let's go.

Deven nodded, his mind focused on the task at hand. He was ready to follow Govind ji into the heart of the mystery that shrouded Shanti Villa, even if it meant leaving behind the security of the idol.

The revelation hung in the air, and Deven's curiosity mixed with a sense of foreboding. Shanti Villa held secrets far more complex and sinister than he had ever imagined.

Chamber of Shadows

As they began to ascend the staircase leading to the upper floor, Deven couldn't escape the palpable sense of unease that gripped him. His heart pounded faster with each step, and his mind raced with thoughts of the eerie footprints and handprints he had discovered earlier. Those distinct marks were now unmistakably linked to the four unfortunate souls who had once lived happily within the walls of Shanti Villa. Their tragic fate had transformed them into sinister entities, and they had beckoned to Deven, attempting to draw him into their darkness.

Deven couldn't help but wonder why Govind ji had taken away the Krishna Idol, which had provided him with a sense of comfort and protection during his previous encounters. The absence of his spiritual anchor left him feeling vulnerable. However, he reassured himself that Govind ji was by his side, ready to intervene should anything go awry. His trust in Govind ji was unwavering, and he relied on the guru's wisdom and guidance.

With each step up the stairs, Deven steeled himself for the challenges that awaited them on the upper floor of Shanti Villa.

Deven started his venture to the upper floor of Shanti Villa. Govind ji trailed behind him, their footsteps echoing through the eerie silence of the entrance lobby. It was clear that something sinister had been unleashed; the doors to various rooms lay shattered, and the windows were cracked, evidence of the malevolent forces that had been provoked by Deven's unwavering faith. These entities fed on fear, and Deven's refusal to succumb had left them hungry, desperate to instill terror once more.

As they stepped into the nursery room, a chilling sight awaited them. In the center of the room stood a fifth chair, seemingly placed with deliberate intent. The implications of this discovery sent shivers down Deven's spine. Had these entities anticipated his return, luring him to this very spot? It was a disturbing thought that struck him like a bolt of lightning.

Deven turned to look into Govind ji's eyes, searching for guidance and reassurance. However, Govind ji's face remained eerily expressionless, a silent challenge for Deven to trust his instincts and take the necessary action. The room's oppressive atmosphere seemed to thicken, and Deven knew that a terrifying confrontation was inevitable.

Suddenly, as Deven entered the room, he felt a forceful push from behind that sent him sprawling onto the cold, unforgiving floor. Shock and disbelief coursed through him as he turned to see who had betrayed him. It couldn't be true, could it? Govind ji, his trusted guide and mentor, had just shoved him into this room. A wave of confusion and fear washed over Deven as he grappled with the idea that he had been offered as a sacrificial pawn to these malevolent entities.

Questions swirled in his mind like a maddening tempest. Had his faith in Govind ji been a cruel deception? Was this a sinister plot to appease the evil forces that lurked within Shanti Villa? His trust, so steadfast until now, crumbled into doubt. Deven found himself trapped in a nightmarish scenario, stripped of his only shield—the Krishna Idol, which Govind ji had taken from him. Fear and desperation clawed at his heart as he struggled to make sense of this horrifying betrayal. Panic and fear gripped Deven's heart as he realized he was alone in this dire situation, stripped of his only shield. The room seemed to close in around him, the shadows lengthening, and he knew that he was about to face a terrifying ordeal with no apparent ally by his side.

"Govind ji! Open the door, please! Why are you doing this? What's happening?" Deven's voice cracked with fear as he pleaded for answers that seemed to be swallowed by the oppressive stillness. He tried finding his phone but it was not there in his pockets, it must have been left downstairs. Deven's screams reverberated within the confined space of the room, but the door remained resolutely shut, as if it had absorbed his cries, leaving him in an eerie silence that was more terrifying than any sound. Desperation consumed him, and he continued to pound on the door with all his might, his fists and shoulders taking the brunt of his futile efforts.

His relentless thumping and kicking yielded no results. The door, once solid and imposing, remained immovable, refusing to budge even an inch. Deven finally understood that his struggle was in vain, and a sinking feeling of isolation settled in.

As he scanned the room, he became acutely aware of his dire circumstances. He was trapped in a nightmarish place, abandoned by the one he had trusted the most. The room's atmosphere seemed to thicken with malevolence, and the shadows danced menacingly in the corners. Deven knew he had to find a way out, but the odds were stacked against him, and the true horrors of Shanti Villa were yet to reveal themselves.

Deven's heart raced as he began his meditation, his mind a whirlwind of fear, confusion, and betrayal. With every breath, he sought to calm the storm within. Govind ji's teachings echoed in his thoughts, and he clung to the wisdom he had received.

In the stillness of the room, Deven pictured himself standing strong amid the chaos. He recalled the lessons of Lord Krishna, understanding that the divine would assist those who sought inner truth and made an effort to help themselves. It was a revelation of self-reliance and inner strength.

As he breathed in deeply and exhaled slowly, Deven felt a shift within him. His chakras aligned, and his mind focused. He visualized a radiant light enveloping him, a protective shield forged from the depths of his own courage and faith. He realized that he couldn't rely on Govind ji or external forces to save him; he had to be his own savior.

The room's malevolent aura seemed to lose its grip on him. The oppressive shadows receded slightly, and Deven's confidence grew. He knew that whatever lay ahead in Shanti Villa's twisted reality, he had tapped into a source of strength that no sinister entity could extinguish. With newfound determination, he opened his eyes and took a deep breath, ready to confront the horrors that awaited him.

In the eerie confines of the room, Deven's desperation fueled his determination. He knew there was something hidden behind that sinister wall, and he had no time to waste. As shown on house plan by Govind ji', he had already realized that the room was significantly smaller than the dimensions mentioned. Every echoing knock seemed to pierce the eerie silence, and Deven knew he was onto something, he began knocking on the walls, searching for any hollow spots. It didn't take long before a hollow echo reverberated through the room, confirming his suspicion – there was indeed something concealed within.

The room seemed to react to Deven's investigation. Its malevolent energy stirred, as if disturbed by his relentless determination. Ominous sounds emanated from the very walls he sought to breach, but Deven pressed on, fueled by a resolve that transcended the supernatural.

His gaze fell upon the ominous table, the epicenter of the room's malevolence. Surrounded by the five sinister chairs, it stood as a silent witness to the horrors that had unfolded within these walls. Deven seized the fifth chair, which had seemingly been reserved for him, and wielded it like a makeshift battering ram.

With each bone-chilling impact, the plastered wall began to crumble. The room itself seemed to protest, its dimensions shifting and contorting in response to the disturbance. The unsettling cacophony grew louder, a symphony of dread. Deven's relentless assault continued unabated, even as the chair splintered and shattered under the relentless force.

In an act of desperation, he turned his attention to the mahogany table – the very object that had terrorized Asha ji in her final moments. With grim determination, he hoisted the heavy table, its dark wood laden with sinister history. The room recoiled as if in fear, but Deven's resolve remained unshaken. He was determined to uncover the truth hidden within this nightmarish chamber, no matter the cost.

As Deven reached for the sinister mahogany table, he could feel a growing malevolence in the room. The atmosphere seemed to thicken with dread, as if the very air had turned hostile. The room became oppressively dark, and he could sense an ominous presence surrounding him.

In the shadows, the figures of Asha, Alok, Shanti Devi, and Anand took shape, their once-familiar forms twisted into grotesque, sinister versions of themselves. Their eyes glowed an eerie red, and wicked grins stretched across their faces. The room resonated with their menacing laughter, echoing like a haunting symphony.

Deven's heart raced as he felt their spectral hands attempting to grasp his own, trying to prevent him from lifting the table. Their chilling whispers filled his ears, urging him to abandon his quest, to succumb to the darkness that had consumed them.

But he couldn't back down now. With a surge of determination, he heaved the mahogany table towards the wall with all his might. The wall began to give way, bricks and plaster crumbling to reveal a hidden chamber beyond. The room convulsed in a final, desperate attempt to keep its secrets buried, but Deven pressed on, determined to uncover the truth that had been concealed for far too long.

As Deven broke through the wall with the mahogany table, the hidden chamber was unveiled, revealing a dreadful sight within. Unearthly whispers and malevolent shadows filled the room, swirling around him like a sinister tempest. The eerie entities, Asha, Alok, Shanti Devi, and Anand, surged forward, their spectral forms intent on stopping him. With a collective malevolence, they attacked Deven, clawing at him, and hurling him into the air. He felt powerless, suspended in the dark abyss, his very life at the mercy of these demonic forces. As the wall crumbled before him, revealing the hidden chamber, the malevolent entities lunged at Deven with a ferocity that sent him sprawling across the room. He felt an invisible force lift him off his feet, suspending him in the air like a puppet on strings. The sinister figures circled him, their red eyes burning with malevolence.

Deven's heart pounded in his chest as fear threatened to overtake him. But in the darkest moment of this harrowing battle, he heard a soft, reassuring voice within. It was an inner voice, his own spirit urging him to stand strong, "Deven, get up and align your chakras to enlighten the divine energy from within" said his inner voice, to tap into the newfound divine energy that had awakened within him. He closed his eyes and focused on the chakras he had aligned, finding a deep well of courage and strength.

With newfound determination, Deven summoned the divine energy that pulsed through him. A brilliant light emanated from his very core, engulfing him in a radiant aura acting as his shield. The sinister entities recoiled in agony, their wailing cries echoing through the room.

Guided by the inner voice, Deven began to chant a mantra, his voice clear and unwavering, "ॐ नमो भगवते वासुदेवाय" (Om Namo Bhagavate Vasudevaya). The room quaked with the intensity of his spiritual energy, causing the malevolent entities to falter. The walls seemed to tremble, and the room itself appeared to convulse.

With one final surge of determination, Deven directed the divine energy toward the sinister figures. They screamed and writhed, their forms started dissolving into nothingness, vanquished by the power of his faith and courage. As Deven's divine light and energy enveloped the sinister entities, they let out agonized shrieks that pierced the very fabric of the room. Their forms began to smolder and burn, their wicked visages twisting in torment. The room seemed to shake as if it could no longer contain the clash of forces.

Deven's voice, once soft and unwavering, now echoed and reverberated with an intensity that was unbearable for the malevolent figures. His mantra, "ॐ नमो भगवते वासुदेवाय" (Om Namo Bhagavate Vasudevaya), grew louder and more powerful with each repetition, drowning out the wails of the tormented entities.

The room itself seemed to respond to this celestial battle. Shadows danced wildly on the walls, and the air crackled with energy. Deven's aura expanded, pushing back the malevolent forces and searing them with its divine radiance.

Despite their desperate attempts to resist, the sinister figures could not withstand the overwhelming power of

Deven's faith and inner strength. They burnt into ashes and disintegrated into nothingness slowly, their cries fading into an eerie silence.

As the last vestiges of the entities vanished, the room settled into an eerie calm. The oppressive atmosphere that had clung to Shanti Villa for so long lifted, replaced by a profound sense of peace. Deven, his body weary but his spirit triumphant, knew that he had vanquished the malevolence that had plagued this place for generations.

The room, once a sanctuary of darkness, was now bathed in the warm, gentle sunlight of a new beginning. Deven had not only conquered the sinister entities but had also reclaimed the place, freeing the tormented souls of Asha, Alok, Shanti Devi, and Anand from their malevolent existence.

The room now stood as a symbol of peace, bathed in the soft light of a new beginning. Deven, drained but triumphant, stepped out into the sunlight, his heart filled with gratitude and his faith reaffirmed. Shanti Villa had been set free from its sinister past, thanks to the courage, faith, and inner strength he had discovered within himself.

As Deven gazed into the hidden chamber behind the broken wall, he was met with a gruesome sight. The room contained the remains of four bodies, three of which had decomposed to the point where only their skeletal remains remained. The fourth body, though slowly decomposing, still bore some semblance of its former self. It was definitely Asha Ji, Poor soul. These were the tormented souls of Asha, Alok, Shanti Devi, and Anand, victims of the malevolent forces that had plagued Shanti Villa for so long.

In the corner of the chamber, Deven discovered a large cupboard, and as he opened its creaking doors, he revealed a cache of ill-gotten wealth. Gold, Land acquisition documents and cash, accumulated through unethical means and hidden away for decades, lay before him. The money, now wasted and decayed, was a stark reminder of the tragic end that befell those who had chosen the path of greed and malevolence. It was a grim testament to the age-old adage that bad karma always attracts its bitter fruits.

Deven's heart was heavy as he looked upon the scene, a poignant reminder of the consequences of one's actions. The acquired wealth hidden in this secret chamber had ultimately led to the downfall of those who had sought to amass them. In this moment of solemn reflection, Deven knew that he had not only cleansed Shanti Villa of its sinister forces but had also uncovered the tragic history that had fueled their malevolence. The past had been laid bare, and it was now time for Shanti Villa to find its true path to peace and redemption.

Deven's eyes, still heavy from the grim scene he had just witnessed, shifted to the door as it slowly creaked open. In the doorway stood Govind Ji, his serene smile contrasting sharply with the horror that filled the chamber. Deven's anger was palpable as he vented his frustration.

"Why did you do this?" Deven's voice trembled with a mixture of anger and hurt. "You left me in the middle of that battle. You pushed me. It feels like betrayal, Govind Ji."

Govind Ji's smile remained unwavering as he met Deven's gaze. "My dear Deven," he began, "sometimes, we must confront the darkness within ourselves to truly banish the external shadows. You had the strength within you all along, but you needed to discover it for yourself. I did not abandon you; I simply gave you the space to realize your own power. Your faith and courage brought you through this battle. You've emerged stronger and wiser."

Govind ji's smile remained serene, his eyes reflecting a deep understanding of Deven's anger and confusion. He stepped forward and gently placed a hand on Deven's shoulder.

"Deven," he began softly, "I understand your feelings, and I apologize for the pain I caused you. But sometimes, the path to wisdom is not a straight one. It's filled with challenges, tests, and moments of isolation. You see, what you faced today was not just a battle with external forces but a battle within yourself. I had to test your resolve, your faith, and your courage. You had to confront your deepest fears and doubts."

Deven, still brimming with anger and frustration, looked at Govind ji, seeking answers to the burning questions in his mind. "But why, Govind ji? Why did you push me into this on my own"

Govind ji's gaze was compassionate, his voice filled with wisdom. "Because, my dear Deven, in this journey of self-discovery and spiritual awakening, there will be times when you must stand alone to truly understand your strength. I had faith in you, but you needed to find faith in yourself. The divine power that guides us is within you, and today, you harnessed it with your own will and determination. You broke through the darkness and emerged victorious."

As Govind ji spoke these words, Deven felt a weight lifting from his shoulders. He began to realize the profound lesson hidden within the trials of the day. It was a lesson of self-reliance, faith, and the inner strength that resided in each person.

Tears welled up in Deven's eyes as he looked at Govind ji, not with anger but with gratitude. "I understand now, Guruji. This journey is not just about defeating external forces; it's about conquering our own inner demons and discovering our true potential."

Govind ji nodded in approval; his smile now filled with pride. "Exactly, Deven. You've taken a significant step on this spiritual path today, and I am here to guide you, but remember, you are never truly alone. The divine power that resides within you is your constant companion, and it will always light your way."

With these words of wisdom, the two of them exited the chamber of horrors, leaving behind the secrets and darkness of Shanti Villa.

Govind Ji's expression became more solemn as he continued, "The moment I saw Mrs. Asha Devi, I could sense a dark aura around her. Though she may not have been actively involved in the unethical path chosen by Anand Ji her father-in-law, she enjoyed the benefits and profits that came from it. She was even made aware by Shanti Devi her mother-in-law, who apparently was the 1st victim she tried to tell Asha ji how this wealth was acquired but somehow that did not affect her much during her young age. As for Anand Ji, he accumulated this wealth, this land, and all this money on the backs of many people's sufferings. This house was constructed on their curses, and all this jewelry and wealth are cursed. This led to the destruction of his own family. Even Alok, when he found that cash in his father's drawer, had an inkling of what his father had done to acquire this wealth. He chose to spend it in his own comfortable way."

The weight of the past actions and their consequences hung heavily in the air. Deven realized that the curse of their deeds had not only haunted them in life but continued to torment them even in death. It was a stark reminder of the karmic consequences that followed unethical choices.

Govind Ji continued, "So, when Alok Ji disappeared and Asha Ji came to visit me in the Ashram, I saw a dark shadow behind her, I came to know what situation she must be stuck in. I tried to make her understand with what she was truly fighting. However, the burden of guilt weighed down her spirit, overpowering her will to confront the odds. She understood that she had been lured by the promise of wealth and luxury, and her guilt prevented her from gathering the courage to resist. She slowly withdrew from the path of righteousness, and a few years later, she disappeared as well. It was then that you came into the picture, Deven."

Govind Ji's eyes sparkled with admiration as he continued, "You had an immense positive light and aura around you. When we began talking, you revealed how you had lost your parents and were miraculously saved. Even in your innocence, you possessed unwavering faith in God. You were untouched by the allure of wealth and comfort you received in inheritance, choosing instead to take up someone else's battle. You are a shining example of courage and selflessness."

He paused; his voice filled with conviction. "In the Bhagavad Gita, Lord Krishna teaches us that 'Mann,

Vachan, and Karma,' when aligned, result in true courage that ultimately leads to victory. When a person's thoughts, words, and actions are in harmony, it gives birth to divine power, self-belief, and courage. Today, Deven, you have experienced the manifestation of this divine power within you."

Deven's eyes shimmered with a newfound understanding as he absorbed Govind Ji's words. He felt a profound shift within himself, as if the very core of his being had been touched by the divine. He heard his inner voice, now clearer and more resolute than ever before, guiding him on a path of courage and selflessness. With deep sincerity, he asked the question that had been lingering in his heart, "But Govind Ji, why did you push me into that battle alone? You could have easily Accompany me then Why did you orchestrate all of this?"

Govind Ji met Deven's gaze with a serene smile, his eyes reflecting the wisdom of ages. In a gentle but firm tone, he replied, "Deven, my dear child, the journey of self-discovery and courage is one that you must undertake alone. While guidance and support can light your way, it is you who must walk the path. I did not push you into that battle to betray you, but to help you find the strength that already resided within you. Sometimes, it is in the darkest moments of solitude that we uncover our true potential. You have given birth to something divine within yourself today, and for that, you needed to face this trial. Remember, Deven, you are never truly alone, for the divine always walks beside those who seek truth and righteousness."

Deven felt a profound sense of gratitude and acceptance wash over him. He now understood that this journey was not just about defeating external evil but also about conquering the inner doubts and fears that had held him back. His trust in Govind Ji had deepened.Tears of gratitude welled up in Deven's eyes as he realized the profound significance of Govind Ji's guidance and wisdom. In this spiritual battlefield of Shanti Villa, Govind Ji had become his charioteer, his Sarthi, just as Lord Krishna had guided Arjuna on the battlefield of Kurukshetra. Deven bowed deeply before Govind Ji, his heart filled with reverence and humility, seeking his blessings for the challenges that lay ahead. It was a moment of deep spiritual connection, where the student acknowledged the divine presence of his teacher, his Guru.

After the emotional and enlightening encounter in the eerie depths of Shanti Villa, Govind Ji and Deven shared a heartfelt hug. Yet, Govind Ji was quick to bring them back to the practical aspects of the situation.

"Deven," he began, "I have already called the police. It's essential that we conduct the final rites for the Joshi family respectfully. Their spirits have suffered long enough. Now, we need to help them find peace. We must cooperate fully with the authorities, allowing them to handle the investigation professionally. This will not only provide closure to the missing person's cases but also give the Joshi family the dignity they deserve."

Deven nodded, understanding the importance of this final act of compassion and closure. Together, they awaited the arrival of the authorities, prepared to do what was necessary to bring peace to the restless spirits that had haunted Shanti Villa for so long.

Soon, the police arrived at Shanti Villa. They conducted a thorough investigation, sealing the place off from the curious onlookers. The hidden gold and cash were carefully collected as evidence, ensuring that the ill-gotten wealth would no longer haunt anyone. The bodies of the Joshi family were sent for postmortem, providing some closure to the long-standing mystery and the missing persons' cases.

Later that day, As Govind ji dropped Deven off at his apartment, he turned to him with a warm smile. "Deven, I want you to join me for Satsang this evening after you've rested enough. Your presence would be most welcome."

Deven nodded, his gratitude shining in his eyes. "Thank you, Guruji. I wouldn't miss it for anything. "With that, he stepped out of the car, feeling a renewed sense of purpose and a deep connection to the spiritual path that had unexpectedly unfolded before him.

CHAPTER TEN

A New Purpose

Deven slept like a baby that day, his exhausted body and mind finding solace in deep slumber. He didn't even eat; the events of the previous night had left him physically and emotionally drained. As he slowly stirred awake around 5 in the evening, he felt a mix of weariness and determination.

He got up, stretched his body, and then proceeded to take a refreshing shower. The warm water helped ease some of the tension that had built up within him. Afterward, he prepared his favorite coffee, savoring each sip as it brought a sense of comfort and familiarity.

With the evening sun casting long shadows, Deven checked his watch. It was time. He called an Uber, knowing he had a date with destiny at the ashram. Today, the lessons of courage, faith, and selflessness he had learned in Shanti Villa would continue to guide him on his spiritual journey.

When Deven arrived at the ashram, he noticed that the Satsang had already started. The serene atmosphere of the place welcomed him, and the people gathered there seemed to wear calm expressions on their faces. The gentle hum of spiritual discourse filled the air, soothing his soul.

As the Satsang continued, Deven watched in admiration as individuals shared their thoughts, questions, and concerns with Govind ji. They sought guidance and wisdom to navigate the challenges in their lives. It was a beautiful and humbling sight, witnessing how Govind ji's teachings and presence could provide solace and direction to those in need.

Deven settled into his seat, grateful for the opportunity to be a part of this community of seekers. He knew that, like those around him, he too had found a path toward self-discovery and spiritual growth, guided by the wisdom of his guru, Govind ji.

Later Govind ji asked Deven to join for his green tea, As Deven and Govind ji strolled through the peaceful ashram corridors, the aroma of green tea filled the air. Deven gathered the courage to share something that had been brewing in his heart.

"Govind ji," he began, "I have made a decision. Under your guidance, I have found a treasure greater than any material wealth—a newfound awakening within me, a second chance at life. I've realized that my interests in this material world have waned, and I want to dedicate myself to a higher purpose."

Govind ji looked at Deven with his characteristic gentle gaze, silently encouraging him to continue.

Deven continued, "I want to establish a trust and an NGO in the name of Mrs. Asha Devi. I hope you would agree to be the trustee and founder of this organization. The wealth from Shanti Villa, along with the house itself, should be used for a greater cause. I believe that by doing so, we can provide closure to the Joshi family and help absolve the curses that have haunted Shanti Villa for years. Additionally, this act can bring peace and benefit to many other people in need."

Govind ji nodded thoughtfully, acknowledging the weight of Deven's decision. He placed a reassuring hand on Deven's shoulder and spoke with a serene wisdom that had guided so many on their spiritual journeys.

"Deven, my dear," he began, "I commend your compassion and your eagerness to make a difference in the world. It is indeed a significant decision, and it warms my heart to see you taking such a noble path. However, I want you to know that the house is now free from the curses and dark shadows that once plagued it. The spiritual battle you fought, and the divine energy you harnessed, have cleansed that space."

He continued, "While establishing the trust and NGO in Mrs. Asha Devi's name is a beautiful idea, there's no need to rush into this decision. You have the opportunity to do many things with the property and inheritance. The wealth is not an easy thing to give away like this, there are chances that you might regret this decision later. Take your time to consider what aligns best with your newfound purpose and the greater good you wish to achieve."

"You're right, Govind ji," Deven replied with gratitude in his voice. "I understand that the house is now free from the darkness that once consumed it.. There's much we can do to honour the Joshi family's memory and make a positive impact on the world. He continued, but one thing is clear, I want to ensure that the wealth and resources that have come into my possession are only to be used for the betterment of others. In whatever way I choose to proceed, your guidance will remain invaluable to me, and I'd be honoured if you'd consider being a part of this endeavour."

Deven's eyes held a determination and newfound purpose as he spoke. The experiences at Shanti Villa had transformed him, and he was ready to embark on a new path, guided by his inner light and Govind ji's wisdom.

Govind ji smiled, his eyes reflecting pride in Deven's thoughtful and measured approach. "Deven, my dear," he said, "I have no doubt that you will make the right choices, and I'll be here to assist you every step of the way.

Deven now had to resume his normal life, Deven's morning routine had indeed evolved. He woke up early, greeted the rising sun with a peaceful 'Namaste' from his balcony, and then proceeded to take a refreshing shower. Afterward, he performed his daily meditation, aligning his chakras and centering his mind for the day ahead.

The addition of the Krishna idol in his pooja was a constant reminder of the divine energy he had discovered within himself. With reverence, he lit incense and offered fresh flowers and prasad to the idol, seeking blessings for the day.

After completing his spiritual practice, Deven transitioned into the bustling world of corporate Pune life, carrying with him the newfound perspective and strength he had gained from his extraordinary journey.

As Deven returned to his office after almost two weeks, he couldn't help but feel like a stranger in a familiar land. Everything around him seemed different, as if he had stepped into an alternate reality. The once-familiar faces of his colleagues wore new expressions, and the hustle and bustle of corporate life felt like a distant memory.

He moved through the office, noticing changes in the workspace layout, new faces among his coworkers, and a different energy in the air. It was as though his perspective had shifted, and he was now seeing his professional life through a different lens.

Despite the changes, Deven remained calm and composed, carrying the newfound wisdom and courage he had gained from his extraordinary experiences. This transformation had not only altered his personal life but was now beginning to shape his approach to work and the world around him.

As Deven settled at his desk and switched on his laptop, his usual routine kicked in. However, as he began to review his emails, his heart sank. There, at the top of his inbox, were several complaint emails from one of his most significant clients. The subject lines were glaring in red, and the urgency of the matter was evident.

The client was furious, and the tone of the emails was aggressive. They had discovered a critical software bug that had caused disruptions in their operations, and they had escalated the issue to upper management. Deven realized that he had forgotten to assign this client's concerns to a colleague before his unexpected absence, and this oversight had resulted in a significant problem.

As he read through the emails, he felt a familiar pressure building in his chest. This was the kind of situation that would usually have him stressed and anxious, but something had changed within him. The courage and resilience he had discovered in the face of supernatural challenges were now being tested in his professional life.

Deven took a deep breath and dialled Mr. Sethi's number. The phone rang a few times before a sharp, authoritative voice answered.

"Mr. Sethi, this is Deven from TechPro Solutions. I sincerely apologize for the issues you've been facing with our software," Deven said, his voice filled with genuine concern.

Mr. Sethi replied, his tone still quite stern, "Deven, this has caused us significant disruptions. Our operations are at a standstill. This is unacceptable."

"I understand, Mr. Sethi, and I take full responsibility for this oversight," Deven replied earnestly. "I'd like to make it right. Can I come to your office personally to discuss the issue, understand your requirements better, and provide a solution that ensures this doesn't happen again?"

There was a brief pause on the other end of the line, and then Mr. Sethi replied, "Very well, Deven. Come to our office today around 5PM. We need this sorted out urgently."

Deven nodded, even though the client couldn't see it over the phone. "Thank you, Mr. Sethi. I promise you; we'll resolve this matter promptly."

With that, the conversation ended, and Deven knew he had a challenging day ahead. Deven hung up the phone, knowing that he had a lot of work to do to prepare for his meeting with Mr. Sethi. He quickly gathered his team to discuss the issue and assigned tasks to address the software bug. Despite the urgency of the situation, Deven remained calm and composed, drawing on the inner strength and resilience he had discovered during his harrowing experiences at Shanti

Villa.

As the day wore on, Deven worked diligently with his team to identify the root cause of the problem and devise a solution. He found himself more focused and determined than ever before, driven by a newfound sense of purpose. The hours passed quickly, and by the time he left the office that evening, he had a comprehensive plan in place to resolve the client's issues.

Deven knew that today's meeting with Mr. Sethi would be a crucial test of his abilities and determination. He was ready to face the challenge head-on, armed with the knowledge that he had conquered even greater obstacles in the past.

Deven arrived at Mr. Sethi's office with a sense of determination. He was prepared to face the consequences of his oversight and to do whatever it took to make things right. As he entered Mr. Sethi's plush office, he could sense the tension in the air.

Mr. Sethi looked visibly angry, and his manager, Mr. Kapoor, appeared equally displeased. They wasted no time in expressing their frustration over the software issues and the negative impact it had on their operations. Deven apologized sincerely, acknowledging the gravity of the situation.

However, it seemed that Mr. Sethi and Mr. Kapoor were not in a forgiving mood. They expressed their disappointment and even mentioned that they were considering disassociating their company from Deven's firm due to the repeated problems they had faced

As Mr. Sethi leaned forward, frustration etched across his face, in that moment something unusual happened. Deven suddenly found himself slipping into an almost trance-like state. It was as if time had slowed down, and he could see Mr. Sethi's lips moving, but the words seemed distant and muted.

In this surreal moment, an automatic response emerged from Deven's mouth, his voice steady and commanding. He said, "Mr. Sethi, please ask Mr. Kapoor to leave the cabin right now. I need to speak with you privately."

The transformation in Deven's demeanour was so sudden and compelling that it left Mr. Sethi utterly speechless. His aura seemed to carry an undeniable authority, and his words bore a weight that compelled Mr. Sethi to obey without question. He turned to Mr. Kapoor and instructed him to leave the room immediately, leaving the two of them alone in the cabin.

Deven, still in this strange, trance-like state, continued to gaze at the crystal showpiece on Mr. Sethi's table. He spoke in a measured, almost ethereal tone, "Mr. Sethi, I sense there may have been health and family issues plaguing your life lately. Has there been any unrest?"

Mr. Sethi's eyes widened with astonishment, his face a mix of disbelief and bewilderment. He stammered, "Mr. Deven, what on earth are you talking about? Are you in your right mind? We're here to discuss the software issue. Why are you going off-topic?"

Deven remained unnervingly calm, his eyes fixed on the crystal. "You must remove that crystal showpiece from your cabin. Whoever gifted it to you doesn't have your best interests at heart. Also, if possible, try practicing 11 Surya Namaskars every morning after you wake up. On a different note, the software issue has been resolved, and you won't face any inconvenience moving forward."

The atmosphere in the room was charged with an inexplicable energy. Deven's body trembled as if an electric current was coursing through him, channelling his energy in a mysterious and powerful way. Mr. Sethi's anger and scepticism seemed to evaporate in the face of Deven's enigmatic presence.

Deven, abruptly shaken from his trance-like state, finally tore his gaze away from the crystal showpiece and looked at Mr. Sethi, who was still staring at him in sheer astonishment. With an air of urgency, Deven said, "I must take my leave now, Mr. Sethi."

He hastily left Mr. Sethi's office, his mind racing with a mix of confusion and anxiety. Deven summoned an Uber as he stepped out of the building; the sun was beginning to set, casting long shadows across the city. All he could think of was the need to share this bewildering experience with Govind ji in person.

As Deven reached the Ashram, the Satsang was winding down. He spotted Govind ji in his customary cheerful demeanour, surrounded by devotees. With an affectionate pat on Deven's back, he welcomed him warmly.

"Ah, my boy, I'm delighted to see you here today," Govind ji greeted him, his eyes twinkling with mischief. "You look a bit exhausted. Come, let me make some green tea for you. But hold your horses till then," he chuckled, sensing that Deven had something important to share.

Deven nodded, feeling a mix of anticipation and anxiety. The events of the day, from his strange encounter with Mr. Sethi to the unexplainable trance-like state, had left him with a profound sense of wonder and curiosity. As Govind ji prepared the tea, Deven knew he was about to embark on another insightful conversation that would reshape his understanding of the world around him.

Sitting across from Govind ji in the tranquil surroundings of the Ashram, Deven recounted every detail of the perplexing incident at Mr. Sethi's office. Govind ji listened attentively, his wise eyes reflecting a serene understanding. He wore a gentle smile throughout the conversation, as if he had anticipated Deven's transformation all along.

After Deven finished speaking, Govind ji leaned back in his chair, his smile ever-present. He spoke with an air of deep wisdom, "Deven, my dear, why are you so surprised now? Can't you see? Your life has been an incredible journey, marked by resilience and unwavering faith. You've faced life-threatening situations and escaped death twice in your life and emerged stronger because of your unbreakable faith and your inherently ethical and positive mindset. The divinity inside you has awakened, and it will continue to guide not only you but also those fortunate enough to be around you. Spiritual awakening opens your senses to a world beyond the ordinary, allowing you to perceive and experience things that elude most. Your experiences have transformed you into an extraordinary human being, a blessing in disguise."

Deven gazed into Govind ji's radiant eyes. The Ashram seemed to exude an aura of spirituality and enlightenment, and in that moment, Deven realized that his journey was far from over. It was just the beginning of a new chapter, one where he would continue to discover the depths of his inner divinity and its profound impact on the world around him.

As days turned into weeks, Deven's transformation became even more pronounced. His colleagues, who had once seen him as just another team member, now regarded him with newfound respect. His calm demeanor and unwavering positivity in the face of challenges were inspiring. Deven had become a confidant and mentor to many of his juniors, offering guidance and support with a warm smile.

Even his superiors began to recognize his remarkable qualities. They started consulting him on a wide range of matters, from project strategies to team management. Deven's insights were not just valued; they were sought after eagerly. His office had become a hub of positivity and innovation, and it was clear that his influence was extending beyond the confines of his immediate team.

Deven's journey had not only transformed his own life but had also created a ripple effect, touching the lives of those around him. The divinity that had awakened within him was now radiating outward, making him a beacon of light and wisdom in the corporate world.

Deven was sitting at his desk, having lunch when he noticed his phone flashing with an incoming call from Mr. Sethi. Surprised, he picked up the call and answered, trying to maintain a light and friendly tone, "Yes, Mr. Sethi? I hope that software bug hasn't been troubling you anymore."

Mr. Sethi's voice on the other end sounded composed but with a hint of seriousness, "Deven, can you please come down? I'm sitting in the lounge area just outside your office. I need about 15 minutes of your time."

Deven's curiosity piqued as he wondered what might have prompted Mr. Sethi's call. The last time they had spoken, it had been a tense and unpleasant conversation. Now, it seemed Mr. Sethi had something important to discuss, and Deven couldn't help but wonder what it might be.

Deven was surprised by Mr. Sethi's request. Just a few weeks ago, they had been at odds over a software issue, and now Mr. Sethi was asking for his time. Nevertheless, Deven agreed and told him he would be down in a few minutes.

As he entered the lounge area, he saw Mr. Sethi sitting in one of the plush chairs, looking somewhat different from their last meeting. His demeanor was calmer, and there was a hint of curiosity in his eyes.

"Mr. Sethi, you wanted to see me?" Deven asked as he approached.

Mr. Sethi nodded and motioned for Deven to take a seat. "Yes, please, have a seat. I wanted to talk to you about something important."

Deven settled into a chair, wondering what this meeting could be about. It was clear that Mr. Sethi had something on his mind, something beyond the software issue they had resolved.

Mr. Sethi took a deep breath and began, "Deven, I must admit, I was furious with you the last time we met. B ut something strange happened in my office that day."

Deven raised an eyebrow, intrigued. "What happened?"

Mr. Sethi leaned forward; his voice lowered as if sharing a secret. "When you entered my office that day, it was as if a different energy came with you. You said things, Deven, things that no one else could have known. You spoke about my health, my family issues, and that crystal showpiece on my table. It was all true, and it left me bewildered."

Deven's eyes widened in surprise. He hadn't expected Mr. Sethi to bring up their previous encounter, especially not in this context.

Mr. Sethi continued, "After you left, I couldn't stop thinking about it. I removed that crystal showpiece from my office, as you suggested. And I did those Surya namaskars as well. You won't believe it, Deven, but my health has improved, and some long-standing family issues seem to be resolving themselves."

Deven was taken aback. He had merely mentioned those things on a whim during their previous meeting, guided by some inner voice he couldn't explain. He hadn't expected Mr. Sethi to take his words so seriously.

Mr. Sethi smiled, a mix of gratitude and wonder in his eyes. "Deven, I don't know what you are or how you do it, but you have a unique gift. You've changed something within me." Deven, still surprised by Mr. Sethi's words, replied cautiously, "I... I don't know how to explain it, Mr. Sethi. It was as if something came over me."

Mr. Sethi continued, "Well, Deven, I consulted with a few experts after our last meeting, and they mentioned something about people who possess unique abilities. Abilities to tap into the unknown. They call them 'gifted ones.'"

Deven was taken aback. He had never considered himself gifted in any way.

Mr. Sethi smiled warmly, "Deven, you see, I've been dealing with some health issues that I've kept private. What you told me about removing that crystal showpiece from my cabin and doing Surya namaskar has had a miraculous effect on my well-being. My health has improved remarkably since then."

Deven was humbled by Mr. Sethi's words. It was a surreal moment, one that seemed to reaffirm the extraordinary changes he had experienced in his life.

Mr. Sethi continued, Deven, I am going to ask you one more favor, and I know only you could guide me, so apparently, I am facing certain issues and I feel someone's negative energy has affected my life, the crystal was also gifted by that certain someone, the effect has been now over but I know that certain someone won't stop until he destroys me personally and professionally completely.

Deven listened intently, a sense of intrigue growing within him. He had faced the supernatural and spiritual realms in his recent experiences, but this was a whole new dimension. Deven was stunned. This twist in his life's journey was beyond anything he could have imagined. His life, once ordinary, had transformed into something truly extraordinary, guided by faith, divinity, and the unknown powers within him.

Mr. Sethi continued, "Deven, I want to learn how to protect myself from such negative influences, and I want to understand the source of this dark energy. Will you help me, guide me in this journey to safeguard my life and well-being?

In that very moment, as Deven looked into Mr. Sethi's eyes filled with desperation and hope, he knew that this was his next assignment, his new purpose in life. He had crossed the boundaries between the known and the unknown, journeyed through the realms of fear and courage, and emerged with newfound powers and insight. Deven realized that he was meant to use these gifts to help those who had been trapped in the dark realm, to guide them toward the light, and to protect them from the malevolent forces that lurked in the shadows.

With a deep sense of determination, Deven embraced his destiny. His life had transformed into a spiritual odyssey, and he was now a beacon of light in a world filled with darkness. Together with Mr. Sethi, he would embark on a journey of self-discovery, healing, and redemption, knowing that their path would be fraught with challenges, but also with the promise of enlightenment and liberation.

As they set out on this new adventure, Deven couldn't help but wonder what other mysteries and revelations awaited him in the uncharted territory of the spiritual realm. One thing was certain – he was no longer an ordinary man leading an ordinary life. He had become a spiritual warrior, a guardian of light, and a beacon of hope for those in need.

To Be Continued.....